## One prom date, coming up . . .

"I want you to help me transform *me,* a super-plain Jane, into the kind of girl that you and your friends would go for."

Max's jaw was practically on the floor. "*Transform* you?"

"Yes," I said firmly. "I'm tired of being a geek. I want to be that *other* kind of girl—the kind that could theoretically be popular."

Max smiled. Then he frowned. Then he smiled again. "Jane, don't you think you should ask a girl to help you with this . . . transformation? I mean, I don't know anything about . . . feminine . . . stuff."

I shook my head. "No way. I need a guy's point of view. Like, I need to know what kind of clothes *attract* a guy. And what kind of hair." I was really warming up now. "I want a guy to tell me about music and body language, the laugh, the walk, the talk—everything."

"But Jane, you look fine the way you are," Max told me when he got a chance to slide a word in edgewise. "You don't need to change."

I laughed. "Listen, Max," I said to him, staring straight into his eyes. "Would *you* go for me?"

Prom Trilogy

# Max & Jane

## ELIZABETH CRAFT

BANTAM BOOKS
NEW YORK • TORONTO • LONDON • SYDNEY • AUCKLAND

RL: 6, AGES 012 AND UP

MAX & JANE
*A Bantam Book / February 2000*

Cover photography by Michael Segal.

Produced by 17th Street Productions, Inc.
33 West 17th Street
New York, NY 10011.

ISBN: 0-553-49318-3

**Visit us on the Web! www.randomhouse.com/teens**

*Published simultaneously in the United States and Canada*

Bantam Books is an imprint of Random House Children's Books, a
division of Random House, Inc. BANTAM BOOKS and the rooster
colophon are registered trademarks of Random House, Inc. Bantam Books,
1540 Broadway, New York, New York 10036.

PRINTED IN THE UNITED STATES OF AMERICA

OPM    0 9 8 7 6 5 4 3 2 1

*To Grandpa Winfrey, in loving memory*

# One

## Jane

*HOPELESS. ABSOLUTELY HOPELESS.* I stared at myself in the tarnished mirror that hung over the sink in the girls' bathroom. And I didn't like what I was seeing. There might as well have been a sign hanging over my head that read Jane Smith, the Queen of Blah.

"Mirror, mirror, on the wall, who's the dullest of them all?" I whispered to my reflection.

"You are," I answered myself without a moment's hesitation.

I wasn't disfigured or anything. But my looks had the overall personality of a paper towel. Straight, dirty-blond hair, boring blue eyes, and distinctly *un*kissable lips. As for fashion . . . Let's just say that my idea of dressing up was wearing my "good" blue jeans and a T-shirt sans ketchup stains. All in all,

Plain Jane Smith was no one to get excited about.

*I am the last girl in this school who Charlie Simpson would ask out on a date,* I mused as I inspected my teeth in the mirror for signs of renegade poppy seeds from the bagel I had eaten this morning.

Charlie Simpson. Even *thinking* his name made a tingle travel from the tips of my toes to the top of my spine. Charlie was, for lack of a better term, my dream guy. Yes, he was tall, dark, and handsome. He was also one of the most popular guys in school. I doubted there was a girl in all of Union High who wouldn't be psyched to have Charlie slip his leather varsity letterman's jacket around her shoulders on a chilly fall evening.

I leaned close to the mirror, peering at several blackheads that were the current bane of my existence. What would it be like if my skin were as soft and smooth as one of those *Seventeen* magazine cover model's? Or if I had the kind of beauty and style that made guys stop and stare as I walked down a crowded hallway?

*The bell rang for third period. I breezed into Mr. Atkison's classroom, giggling with a couple of cheerleaders. As I slid into my seat, I sensed a pair of electric blue eyes staring at me.*

*"Hi, Charlie,"* I greeted him, batting my foot-long black lashes. *"How's it going?"*

*He ambled toward me, then perched on top of my desk. He was so close that I could smell the sandalwood soap he used in the shower. "Things would be a whole lot better if you would agree to accompany me to our senior prom,"* he answered.

*"I would love to go with you,"* I told him, batting my eyelashes again.

Yeah, right! And I would love to be checked into a mental hospital too. I had been doing my own lame version of batting my eyelashes at Charlie every chance I'd had for the last four years. Ever since I had first seen him, the summer before my freshman year in high school, I'd had an enormous crush on him.

It had been one of the hottest days of August, and I was baby-sitting the Janson twins for what seemed like the thousandth time that summer. To get out of playing yet another hot, sweaty game of kick the can, I took Simon and Ethan to an indoor ice-skating rink. I thought I had found the perfect way to spend the afternoon—until Ethan fell down. He was sprawled out on the ice, wailing and crying.

And then it happened. From the other side of the rink I saw *him* skating toward our little group in strong, smooth glides. The first thing I noticed was his size. He was tall, making the twins and me seem like miniatures in comparison. When he looked at me, his blue eyes twinkled.

He crouched next to Ethan. "What's wrong, Chief?" he asked. "Did you and the ice have a nasty encounter?"

Ethan looked up at this stranger. "Yeah . . ." He was half wailing, half interested in what this guy was going to say next.

The guy looked at me, then at the twins. "I'm

Charlie Simpson," he said. "And I've fallen down on this ice so many times that you'll find imprints of my butt all over this place."

Simon giggled. I giggled. A moment later Ethan's tears stopped, and *he* giggled. "I've only fallen once," he informed Charlie.

Charlie raised his eyebrows. "Once? That's nothing! My kid brother, Bobby, has fallen so many times that I'm beginning to wonder if he knows which way is up!"

A moment later Ethan pushed himself up off the ice. "Let's go, Simon!" he said, the tears gone as suddenly as they had come.

*I'm in love.* It was the first thought that came into my mind. *Charlie isn't only gorgeous, he's a hero.*

"Looks like the little guy is going to live," Charlie commented.

I felt my face turn bright red. This was it. My big moment to flirt with a totally cute guy. "Uh . . . yeah—th-thanks," I stammered.

I wanted to say something witty, something inspired. Instead I stared at my hands and scraped the ice with the tip of my skate blade. *Anything. Say anything,* I ordered myself. *Don't let this opportunity pass you by.*

Suddenly my blade stuck in the ice. "Ahh . . ." I started to pitch forward.

In a flash a pair of strong, warm hands encircled my waist. "Gotcha." Charlie's voice was delightfully low and husky and close to my ear. Instantly most of my body was covered with goose bumps.

"Thanks," I murmured, trying to catch my breath. He had touched me—voluntarily! *Yes!*

Now what? Was I supposed to ask him if he would like to skate around the rink with me? Or maybe I could suggest casually that we gather our charges together and take a hot-chocolate break.

*Yeah, right.* I was usually too shy to ask a stranger what time it was. There was no way I was going to have the guts to ask a perfectly formed member of the male half of the species to join me at the snack bar.

Charlie looked restless. He opened his mouth, and I knew the end of our conversation was at hand. I had to do something drastic. "I'll see you—," he began.

"So, do you, uh, go to Union?" I interrupted before Charlie could make his exit.

He smiled. "I will as of next week. I'm going to be a freshman," he informed me. "You?"

"Same," I answered.

I racked my brain for another question. But the inside of my mouth felt like a cotton ball, and my heart was beating a million beats a minute from having worked up the nerve to ask the *first* question.

In the distance Simon waved at me. "Come *on*, Jane!" he yelled. "Ethan wants to try to skate backward!"

I rolled my eyes. So much for my first attempt at flirting. Duty called. "See you," I said to Charlie.

"Bye, Jane." He turned and skated toward Bobby.

As I headed toward Simon and Ethan, I couldn't help grinning. Okay, so basic shyness had prevented

5

me from getting into a free-flowing conversation with Charlie. At least he knew my name now. There would be plenty of time to work on my flirting skills for future use. After all, I had four years of high school ahead of me!

"Four absolutely *wasted* years," I informed my reflection.

Sure, I had seen Charlie once school had started freshman year. But the first time I caught sight of him, he was standing with a bunch of popular guys that I recognized from junior high. When I walked by the group, Charlie didn't seem to remember me.

That morning I hadn't had the guts to go up and say hi to him. And, four years later, I *still* didn't have the nerve. As far as Charlie Simpson was concerned, the girl from the skating rink didn't exist.

*If only he would notice me,* I thought now, gazing into my boring blue eyes. Where were the fairy godmothers when a girl really needed one? If only some fluttering, floating Tinkerbell type would wave a magic wand and make Charlie fall head over heels for me.

Abracadabra. I would walk into English class, and the air would crackle with electricity. From across the crowded room Charlie would stare at me, his eyes smoldering with passion.

"Jane Smith," he would murmur. "I never realized that *you* are the girl from the skating rink. For four years I've dreamed of this day. . . ."

And then he would ask me to the prom. My fantasy was so real that I found myself smiling into the mirror. I flipped my ponytail and fluttered my eyelashes.

"I would *love* to go to the prom," I murmured softly.

Behind me I heard someone clear her throat. Oh no! My stomach sank to my feet. I bit my lip and spun away from the mirror.

"Excuse *us*, Jane," Rose McNeal announced. "We didn't mean to interrupt."

Rose, along with Madison Embry and Shana Stevens, was standing next to the door of the girls' bathroom. Great! Three of the most popular (and least nice) girls in the senior class had witnessed me being a complete idiot!

I had crashed back into reality in the worst imaginable way. Public humiliation! "Uh . . . gotta go," I mumbled.

A moment later I was out of the bathroom, but I could still hear the girls' giggles as I headed down the hallway. So far this had the makings of one of the worst days of my life!

"I'm aware that some of you enjoyed and understood the subtle themes running through William Faulkner's *As I Lay Dying* more than others," Mr. Atkison commented to our English class forty minutes later. "Luckily for those of you who don't find Mr. Faulkner's writing as easy to digest as an MTV video, you'll have plenty of choices for the topic of your final papers."

I sat up a little straighter in my chair, snapping to attention. I was one of those made-to-order students who obsess about homework, deadlines, and bibliographies. The words *term* and *paper* switched on my note-taking autopilot.

I carefully wrote down the names of American authors we could choose to research for our papers as Mr. Atkison rattled them off. Ernest Hemingway, Nathaniel Hawthorne, Flannery O'Connor. The list went on and on.

When Mr. Atkison stopped talking to take a breath, I shook out my hand and flexed my fingers. Two rows ahead of me, one desk to the right, Charlie Simpson was sketching on an otherwise blank piece of notebook paper. Even from my vantage point I could see that the drawing was a caricature of Mr. Atkison—his mouth oversized and a huge piece of chalk in his hand.

I smiled. Charlie wasn't only drop-dead gorgeous, he was funny. As Charlie passed the sketch to Jack Lacey, I imagined a different life for myself. One in which Charlie passed his drawing to *me*. I would smile, giggle a little, then gently admonish him for being a tad insensitive.

Later we would discuss our English-paper topics in a quiet corner of the library. And then our eyes would meet over a copy of *The Sun Also Rises*. Charlie would lean toward me. . . . *I closed my eyes. A moment later I felt the soft touch of his warm lips against mine. The kiss deepened, and the library around us faded into nothing. . . .*

I sighed, imagining that same kiss under the strobe light at the prom. The thought of walking into the senior prom on Charlie Simpson's arm made me ache. *But that will never happen,* I reminded myself. *Not unless I experience a miracle.*

"The deadline is *not* flexible, folks," Mr. Atkison announced. "I know I've been soft in the past, but I'm serious this time."

Well, one thing was certain. I would have absolutely no trouble getting my paper done on time. Girl-without-a-life Jane Smith had nothing better to do than pore over research books and run spell checks.

As the bell rang, I took a last look at Charlie and resigned myself to the obvious truth: I was hopeless.

# TWO

## Jane

"ICE BLUE IS definitely the 'in' color this spring," Nicole Gilmore commented over a plate of limp green salad. "Practically every prom dress advertised in *Teen People* is silk, strapless, and blue."

I was sitting with Nicole and Christy Redmond, my two best friends, at our usual lunch table. At the moment we were complaining about magazine models and the stuff that passed for food in the Union High cafeteria.

Christy peered over Nicole's shoulder and glanced at the magazine spread. "Do you think that model has breast implants?" she wondered aloud. "Her chest looks like a flotation device."

I glanced down at my own terminally flat chest. Nope. No plastics in this seventeen-year-old torso.

I was as flat as the proverbial pancake.

Nicole handed the *Teen People* to Christy and flipped open what was by now a well-worn copy of *Seventeen*. "Then again, there's a lot of shocking pink featured in *Seventeen*," she commented. "Maybe we have more fashion options than I originally thought."

I speared a piece of macaroni and popped it into my mouth. Ugh. Why couldn't every day be pizza day?

Nicole turned the page and pointed at yet another dress (this one pale lavender with spaghetti straps). "Now, *that's* pretty," she declared.

I didn't bother commenting. Prom dresses. Corsages. Boutonnieres. And then there were this year's most popular prom themes—an evening in Paris, Mardi Gras, a cruise down the Nile. The editors of this month's slew of magazines seemed to have one-track minds. And all of it was making me slightly sick to my stomach.

"Isn't there anything *useful* in those magazines?" I asked my best friends. "Something along the lines of 'Ten Great Ways to Spend Prom Night—Alone!'"

Christy groaned. This wasn't the first time during the last hour that I had referred to my always dateless status. But hey, I wasn't afraid to admit that I had the wallflower market cornered.

"Jane, why don't you just *ask* him to go to the prom with you?" Christy asked.

"Ask who?" I squeaked. Blood immediately rushed to my face.

Nicole set the magazine onto the grimy table. "Duh. Charlie Simpson, your one and only."

11

Unfortunately I couldn't will the blush on my face away. There was no point in denying my crush on Charlie. Nicole and Christy knew better than anyone else that I had fallen hard for the guy. How many times had I bored them with the ice-skating-rink story?

"Oh, right," I answered. "I'll just walk up to one of the most popular, best-looking guys in the school and calmly beg him to accompany me to his senior prom."

"No one said anything about *begging*," Nicole insisted. "We just suggested that you *ask* him."

I pushed the plate of macaroni as far away from me as I could. My appetite was gone. "We all know that's not going to happen," I told my friends. "If I asked Charlie Simpson to the prom and the news got around school, I would be in for some major humiliation."

Christy leaned over and squeezed my hand. "Well, maybe someone else will ask you to the prom. Then you can dance with Charlie while you're there."

"Forget it. I plan to stay home on prom night and watch a *Wonder Years* marathon on Nick at Night." This conversation was seriously bumming me out. With every sentence I uttered, I became even more excruciatingly aware that I had no chance with Charlie.

Nicole took a long swallow from her can of diet Coke, then looked thoughtful for a moment. "Personally, I don't understand what all the fuss over prom is about. The whole thing is like New Year's Eve—pure, overwhelming pressure to get a date and have a good time." She wrinkled her nose. "Who needs it?"

Nicole sounded sincere. But I couldn't help wondering if she would change her mind about going to the prom if some cute guy asked her.

"What about you, Christy?" I asked our other friend. "Do you think Nathan is going to pop the *p* question?"

Christy and Nathan Evert had gone out a few times, but every time we asked her if he was potential boyfriend material, she would shrug noncommittally. At this point it was sort of hard to picture the two of them slow dancing cheek to cheek and gazing into each other's eyes.

"I *hope* Nathan comes through with the invite," Christy replied. "My mom has dreamed about seeing me in a prom dress since I was, like, three years old. I know it would mean a lot to her to have the chance to see her dream become a reality."

A heavy silence fell over the table as the three of us thought about Christy's words. Mrs. Redmond had been sick for a long time now. Although Christy refused to talk about her mother's illness, Nicole and I knew that the fear of her mom's possible death was never far from Christy's mind.

"All of this talk about the prom and slinky, let-it-all-hang-out prom *dresses* is making me want to eat one of those mondo pieces of chocolate cake that the lunch ladies have prepared for our dining pleasure," Nicole said finally, breaking the silence. "Are you two going to join me?"

"Definitely," I declared. "And I want ice cream with mine."

I smiled at my friends. So what if Charlie Simpson didn't know I was alive? I had two of the best friends in the world, and that counted way more than some prom date. At least, that's what I tried to tell myself. . . .

Halfway through my seventh-period study hall I had narrowed down the possible authors to research for my English term paper to Flannery O'Connor and Zora Neale Hurston. As I wrote down notes on a fresh sheet of paper, I felt a familiar tingle of excitement. Grade-A nerd that I was, I actually enjoyed schoolwork.

I was sitting in my favorite corner of the library, a sunny spot next to a huge picture window. I could feel the afternoon sun on the back of my shoulders, and I loved the pervasive smell of hardback books. The truth was that there was no place in all of Union High that I felt more comfortable in than the library.

"Hey, Jane." The greeting had come from somewhere behind my left shoulder.

For a split second my heart leaped into my mouth. A low, husky voice—just like the one from my daydream—had whispered into my ear. I glanced up from my book . . . and crashed back into reality for the umpteenth time that day.

"Oh. Hi, Max." I smiled weakly at Max Ziff, feeling like a total fool.

He raised an eyebrow. "Don't sound so excited to see me."

"Sorry . . . I was, uh, pretty engrossed in my work." *And for a moment I allowed myself to believe that you were Charlie Simpson,* I added silently.

"Good. For a second there I thought I smelled bad." Max pulled up a straight-back wooden chair and sat down across from me.

I grinned. Max Ziff wasn't the type of guy who walked the halls of Union High smelling bad. With dark, curly hair and hazel eyes, Max was one of the most popular guys in school. He was also the *only* popular guy (popular *person,* actually) that I managed to converse with in a fairly normal fashion.

Max and I had gone to junior high together, and since we both took a lot of advanced-placement classes in high school, we usually ended up in English, history, and math together. Exchange enough homework assignments with a guy, and eventually he seems more or less like an actual person—not just a popular jock. I just wished that Charlie would talk to me about tests and papers the way that Max did.

Max pulled a notebook from his backpack and opened it to a blank page. "I missed English because I was talking to a college-baseball recruiter," he informed me. "Any chance you'll fill me in on the term-paper topics?"

I shrugged. "Sure."

On a normal day I would have simply handed him my copious notes from English class and left Max to his own devices. But today I had a one-track mind. I *had* to say Charlie's name aloud.

"But why don't you just get the assignment from Charlie Simpson?" I asked, trying to keep the nervous squeak out of my voice. "He's in our class."

Max snorted. "Charlie is an awesome guy, but paying attention in class isn't his forte."

I already knew this information, having watched Charlie sketch Mr. Atkison for fifteen minutes. But I was half hoping that once Max started talking about his friend, he would keep going. Instead Max just looked at me with an expectant expression on his face.

*Oh, right. The assignment.* I pushed my notes in Max's direction. "Here you go. One prime set of notes, coming up."

"Thanks, Jane. You're the best." He uncapped his pen and bent over the page of notes.

Yep. That was me. Good ol' reliable Jane. I was the girl with the killer test scores and the irresistible school-supply organizer. Too bad there wasn't a course for transforming oneself from the ugly duckling to the cool, beautiful, much-sought-after swan. An A in that class could guarantee a date with Charlie.

Max yawned. "Man, I've been exhausted lately," he said, rubbing his eyes. "Between baseball, Shana, and classes, I'm totally overwhelmed."

"Yeah, I know what you mean," I replied. Which was a lie. I had plenty of time for school—too much time, in fact.

Max bit his lip, studying the paper topic. "Wow.

16

This baby is going to be a major pain in the butt," he commented. "Between this and that ten-page history paper we've got to write for Mrs. Renfrow, I don't know how I'm going to manage."

"You'll do fine," I assured Max. "You always ace your classes."

"Yeah, but sometimes I wish I were a geek," he mused. "Then I could whip out papers without being distracted by baseball practice and a girlfriend."

"Even geeks have distractions," I pointed out. "Jocks don't have the market cornered."

Max looked up from the notes. "Oh, sorry . . . I didn't mean—"

I could have finished his sentence for him. *I didn't mean to offend you, Plain Jane Smith, geek of all geeks.* The fact that Max thought I fit into the untouchable geek category was written all over his face.

Great! My negative self-image was officially *not* all in my head. Obviously others had me labeled as a nerd as well.

"Uh . . ." How was I supposed to respond? *Gee, don't think twice about it, Max. I love being called a geek. It's the thing that gets me out of bed in the morning.*

"Anyway, thanks for the info, Jane." He flipped his notebook shut and practically leaped out of his chair. "I'll see you later."

"See you. . . ." My voice trailed off as I watched Max's retreating back.

Part of me wanted to chase after Max and beg him to tell me what I could do to transform myself from geek to nongeek. After all, he was popular. He probably had the magic recipe that separated the prom queens from the wallflowers.

I could just imagine Max's reaction to *that* request. He would run screaming from the library. *Wouldn't he?*

Some of Max's statements replayed in my mind. He was busy. Extremely busy. And he was clearly anxious to get a baseball scholarship to a good college. Which meant that he would do whatever it took to keep his grades up.

My heart sped up as a completely insane idea began to form in my mind. *Do it, Jane,* I told myself. *Take a chance.* What was the worst thing that could happen? *More public humiliation.* Well . . . so what?

I had only one life to live. There was no reason to hold back. In a couple of months I would be a high-school graduate, and I would probably never see any of these people again.

*Go for it!* I told myself, jumping out of my chair. I had to act *now,* or I knew I would wimp out in a major way.

"Max!" I called out in a loud whisper. "Wait up! I've got to talk to you."

I took a deep breath and closed the distance between us. This was it. My own personal moment of truth . . .

# Three

## Jane

*A*M I COMPLETELY *insane?* I asked myself two seconds later. The answer came quickly. *Yes.*

Max stood in the door of the library, waiting politely for me to say whatever it was I had to say.

"Never mind . . . I, uh, thought you forgot your pen."

Max held up his blue ballpoint pen. "Nope. I've got it right here."

I knew I should turn around, hang my head, and go back to my safe, private table in the corner of the library. But my feet seemed rooted to their spot on the stain-resistant gray carpet that covered the library floor.

"Hold on," I exclaimed as Max turned to leave. "I have a proposition for you."

I was acutely aware of the carpet, a hangnail on my

thumb, the chipped paint on the wall next to me. I was also acutely aware of the expression on Max's face.

He looked confused—really, *really* confused. "Uh . . . a proposition?"

I nodded. I couldn't believe the words that were about to come out of my mouth, but I knew there was no going back now.

"I'll write your English paper *and* your history paper for you," I told him. "On one condition."

Max was staring at me, his mouth slightly agape. "Why would you do that?" he asked. "I don't get it."

I cleared my throat, preparing myself to make a reasoned, logical argument that would convince Max to go along with my plan. "Well, as I understand it, doing these papers is going to seriously interfere with some vital parts of your life."

He nodded. "Yeah . . . so?"

"*So,* I'll write the papers for you—if you do something for me." I laced my fingers together and cracked my knuckles.

"Uh . . . what do you want me to do?" Max asked, obviously uncomfortable with the way our conversation was going.

"I want you to help me transform *me,* a super–plain Jane, into the kind of girl that you and your friends would go for."

Max's mouth had been agape before. Now his jaw was practically on the floor. "*Transform* you?"

"Yes," I said firmly. "I'm tired of being a geek. I want to be that *other* kind of girl—the kind that could theoretically be popular."

Max smiled. Then he frowned. Then he smiled again. "Jane, don't you think you should ask a girl to help you with this . . . transformation? I mean, I don't know anything about . . . feminine . . . stuff."

I shook my head. "No way. I need a guy's point of view. Like, I need to know what kind of clothes *attract* a guy. And what kind of hair." I was really warming up now. "I want a guy to tell me about music and body language, the laugh, the walk, the talk—everything."

"But Jane, you look fine the way you are," Max told me when he got a chance to slide a word in edgewise. "You don't need to change."

I laughed. Max sounded so earnest. "Listen, Max," I said to him, staring straight into his eyes. "Would *you* go for me?"

He shrugged. "I don't notice any girl besides Shana."

Shana Stevens. Long blond hair, round blue eyes, cherry red lips. She walked around like she owned the school—in exactly the manner that I wished I could.

"That's my point, Max," I insisted. "I want you to help me become a girl like Shana—a girl who gets a guy's attention and *keeps* it."

For what seemed like an hour (but was probably around twenty seconds) Max didn't say anything. "Even if I agreed to help you with this, uh, project, you writing my papers would be cheating."

I had anticipated that Max might say something along these lines. But I was ready with an answer.

21

"Max, you're a straight-A student. If you had time, you could write the papers yourself."

"True . . ." He seemed tempted. Who wouldn't be?

"The important thing is learning, right?" I asked. He nodded. "Well, once I finish the papers, you can read them. Then you'll have learned something significant about the subject matter."

He sighed. I imagined a cartoon devil sitting on his left shoulder, a cartoon angel sitting on his right shoulder. Each was telling him to give me a different answer.

"Please, Max," I said simply. "This means a lot to me."

Finally Max grinned and stuck out his hand. "It's a deal."

"Thanks." I felt like throwing my arms around him. Instead I reached out and shook his hand.

*Watch out, Charlie Simpson,* I exclaimed silently. *Here comes non-plain-Jane Smith!*

*Three. Eleven. Fourteen.* I spun the combination on my locker, and it popped open. I started pulling out books at random and stuffing them into my backpack. Now that I had two extra papers to write, I was going to have to be more efficient with my schoolwork than ever.

I was also going to be busier than ever. Max and I were enacting Operation Plain Jane (my name for it, not his) right after school. I almost felt like I had an actual date.

Nicole materialized at my side, carrying a backpack

that was noticeably less weighted down than mine was. "Jane, there's a basket of curly fries with your name written on it at the food court."

"We're going to fill ourselves up with junk food and then try to charm the guy at the movie theater to let us in for free," Christy added. She had appeared beside Nicole.

"Sorry, guys, I'm busy." I zipped up my backpack and slammed the door of my locker shut.

"Busy?" Nicole asked. "Don't tell me you need to get a jump start on next week's calculus assignment."

"Actually, I'm about to embark on a major project," I informed my friends. "And it has nothing to do with homework."

Christy wiggled her eyebrows. "Do tell, do tell."

I glanced in either direction down the corridor. The coast was, as they say, clear. "I'm about to enact a plan to try to attract none other than *the* Charlie Simpson," I told them.

Nicole's eyebrows shot up to her forehead. "How? What's the plan?"

I gulped. I loved my friends—and I trusted them—but I wasn't about to tell them the whole truth of my strategy. I didn't need the standard lecture on what a great person I was and how I didn't need to change.

"I can't tell you two the details—yet." I smiled mysteriously and swung my backpack over my shoulder. "But you'll be the first to know if I manage to snag a date with Charlie."

Nicole and Christy looked at each other, then at

me. Finally they grinned. "Just don't do anything we wouldn't do," Christy said.

"And don't get arrested," Nicole added.

"But good luck, Jane," Christy told me, reaching out to squeeze my arm. "If you ask me, Charlie would have to be blind and deaf not to want to go out with you."

"Ditto for me on that sentiment," Nicole added.

"Thanks, *chicas*," I told my friends.

I waited for them to get halfway down the hall before I headed toward Max's locker. Those girls were supportive—but they were also snoopy.

From two locker banks away I saw that Max wasn't alone. He and Shana Stevens were sharing a knee-melting kiss at Max's locker. I paused next to the water fountain to wait for the kiss to end. Max had promised to keep our deal a secret, and I had no intention of announcing my plan of action to his less-than-friendly girlfriend.

Finally the happy couple broke apart. I watched as Shana sauntered down the corridor, her head held high. *That's how I want to feel,* I thought wistfully. *Confident. In love. On top of the world.*

I felt a surge of excitement as I abandoned my post at the water fountain and walked toward Max's locker. If he was half as good a tutor as I hoped he would be, I would be a whole new girl after I got Max's help with my hair, clothes, and banter skills.

Who knew? Maybe I really did still have a shot at getting a date with Charlie. After all, I lived in a world where an ex–professional wrestler had been elected governor of his state. That was proof that something seemingly impossible *could* happen. Even if I didn't get Charlie to ask me to the prom, at least I was taking matters into my own hands (actually, Max's hands). It was worth a try. I knew deep down in the innermost recesses of my geek soul that I wouldn't be able to live with myself if I didn't at least give love a chance.

I didn't want to graduate from high school with an unfulfilled sensation—as if I had been too afraid to go after my deepest wish. And I definitely didn't want to embark on my college career being haunted by what I *didn't* do in high school!

"Jane Smith," Max called out as I neared. "Ready to begin the first afternoon of the rest of your life?"

I laughed. "Reporting for transformation, sir." And with that statement I began my metamorphosis.

Half an hour later I slid into a booth at Jon's Pizza. The cozy restaurant was far enough away from school that Max and I didn't think we would see anyone we knew. The last thing I wanted was for a group of mindless jocks to overhear my "cool" lesson.

Now, watching Max take a seat across from me, I realized that I was already starting to feel slightly transformed. Maybe I wasn't Madison Embry or Shana Stevens . . . but hey, I *was* about to share a pizza with one of the cutest guys in school. The fact that he already had a girlfriend didn't seem terribly important at the moment.

"Jane, can I ask you something before we start

all of this?" Max asked suddenly, his voice serious.

I sipped my glass of ice water, stalling for time. I had a feeling Max was about to attempt some amateur psychoanalysis, and I wasn't sure I was up to it. Then again, if this plan was going to have any kind of success, we had to be able to trust each other. "Sure," I told him. "Ask me anything."

"Can you explain *why* you want this transformation so badly?" he inquired. "I wasn't kidding when I said that I don't think you need to change."

It was a fair question. But putting four years' worth of living in a social vacuum into a speech of twenty-five words or less was more or less impossible. For a couple of seconds I stared at the ice melting in my glass and thought about how to explain being *me* to Max.

"I'm tired of being invisible," I said finally. "Just one time I want to be noticed at Union High."

"What do you mean by invisible?" he asked. "You've got lots of friends; everybody knows who you are."

I shook my head. "Sure, some people know my name because they've asked if they can copy my homework now and then. But they don't *know* me."

Max leaned back against the side of the booth and looked thoughtful. "There are over two thousand people in our school. . . . Who, exactly, are *they?*"

"You know, the popular crowd—the cheerleaders, jocks, the kings and queens of high school." I took a deep breath. *It's about trust,* I reminded myself, determined not to let my own embarrassment stand in the way of making Max understand.

"It's *your* crowd that makes me feel invisible," I continued, looking Max straight in the eyes. "Around you guys I feel about an inch tall. And I'm sick of it. I want to stand out."

"But you *do* stand out," Max insisted. "You stand out in all of your classes. I mean, you're one of the smartest girls in the entire high school."

I rolled my eyes. "Being noticed for my GPA isn't what I have in mind," I told Max. "I want to look and act like the kind of girl that you and your friends would ask to the prom."

There. I had said the *p* word. The seed was planted, and if the universe wanted to respond, I was going to make sure I was prepared when opportunity knocked at my door. I just hoped that Max didn't back out of our deal. He seemed to be wavering.

"I don't understand why you would want to be someone you're not," Max said after a long pause. "Okay, so you're not the most glamorous-looking girl at Union. . . . Who cares? That's just not your personal style."

Easy for him to say. Max had probably had a date every Saturday night since he was a freshman in high school. I doubted that he would be willing to give up being captain of the baseball team in order to join the chess club.

"Look, Max, we shook on this deal," I said firmly. "I appreciate your concern, but I think I know what's best for me."

At that moment a waitress stopped beside our

table. "Are you two ready to order?" she asked.

Max looked at me. "Jane?"

I shrugged. "You order for me," I told him. "It's your first assignment."

"We'll share a large pizza with pepperoni, mushrooms, and olives," he told the waitress. "And we'd like a pitcher of Coke."

"Phew, I thought you were going to order me a salad with dressing on the side," I said to Max after the waitress had left our table. "It seems like most of the popular girls exist solely on yogurt and rice cakes."

"Aha!" Max exclaimed. "This is one of those moments when you *are* lucky to be getting the input of a guy. You see, Jane, most girls think that we males like it when they eat next to nothing and stare longingly at our cheeseburgers and fries."

"But . . . ?" I leaned forward, hanging on his every word.

"*But* we actually hate that. It's much cooler when a girl eats like a normal person. She seems a lot more confident about who she is."

*Interesting.* I was learning already. "Thanks for the tip."

I unzipped my backpack and pulled out a fresh notebook. At the top of the first page I wrote *Transformation 101.* Underneath I carefully listed my first instruction: *1. Eat like a normal person.*

Max laughed. "Jane, your second is this: *Relax!*"

"Huh?" I looked up from the page.

He pointed at my notebook. "You're not

studying for a *test*. You're trying to create a new image for yourself."

"Right," I answered. "And I don't want to miss a word of advice that comes from your mouth. This is way too important."

Again Max laughed. "As your *teacher,* I'm ordering you to put away those notes, Jane Smith. And that's final."

Well, when he put it like that, I didn't have much choice. I flipped the notebook shut and returned it to my backpack. But without the pen and paper in my hand, I felt more nervous than ever.

"Okay. I'm ready." I folded my hands on top of the worn table and waited for Max to begin enlightening me.

"We'll start with the basics," Max said in a professorial tone. "Above all else, the kind of girl that, quote, 'my friends would go for,' unquote, always comes across as relaxed, cool, and casual."

I nodded. "Relaxed. Cool. Casual." I was itching to write it down, but I didn't dare make a move toward my notebook. "Got it."

Max looked a little skeptical. I guessed my clenched fists and ramrod-straight back didn't seem free and easy enough for him. With an effort I forced myself to ease back into the booth and stop white-knuckling the table.

"Here's the tough part," Max continued. "Although you have to come off as relaxed and casual, you must *also* make it clear to the people around you that you're really busy. You have tons of social demands and several interesting activities that consume much of your precious time."

Luckily the waitress returned with our pizza and Coke at just that moment. I was starting to feel a small amount of panic. If these were the basics, what kind of information was I going to have to process when we got to the advanced material?

"I'm getting a little confused," I admitted to Max as I covered a slice of pizza with grated Parmesan cheese.

"Let's say you stop to say hi to someone in the hall," Max began. "Be totally casual about saying hello, and then leave quickly because you've got someplace you have to be." He paused.

I swallowed another bite of pizza, hoping that none of the sauce was dripping onto my chin. "But what if I *want* to hang out with that particular person, no matter how busy I am?" I asked. "Or what if I'm not really all that busy?"

Max stared at me as if I were an alien. I felt like I had an E.T., Phone Home sign on my forehead. "What . . . what did I say?" *Great. Thirty minutes into the transformation he's already labeled me as beyond help.*

Max set down his slice of pizza. A sure sign he was about to say something of great significance. "Jane, you've got to remember that this is all about image. You're not being yourself—you're being a *version* of yourself."

Slowly I was starting to get the picture. What was going on inside me didn't matter. What *did* matter was what I projected to the world at large. If I could get down the right walk, the right talk, and the right laugh, nobody needed to know that I spent some evenings alphabetizing my bookshelves.

I glanced at my watch. "I should probably get going," I told Max. "I have a yoga class in an hour."

Max looked surprised. "You do? Cool!"

I laughed. "No, I don't. But I guess I'm starting to get the hang of this."

"A gold star for my pupil!" Max announced with a grin. "I think there's hope for her after all."

I took an imaginary bow, pleased with myself. Only one lesson and I was already bantering with one of the coolest guys in school. *Of course, Max is different,* I reminded myself. *He's easy to be around.*

Yep. I might be managing to feel relaxed around Max Ziff. But I was still a long way from getting a prom date with Charlie Simpson.

# Four

## Jane

B Y NINE O'CLOCK that night I had spent at least
an hour staring at my history textbook. Now
that I was signed up for four term papers, it was essential that I devote double the time every night to
schoolwork.

On a normal night I would have been absorbed
in this chapter about Watergate, the scandal that
led to Richard Nixon's resignation as president of
the United States. But I couldn't concentrate
tonight. So far I had read the same five paragraphs
about thirty times.

Pizza with Max had been a decidedly auspicious
beginning to my process of transformation. *So far,
so good,* I assured myself. By the time Max and I
paid the bill, I had made him laugh no less than
three times. Not bad for a geek.

"If only I could be as comfortable with Charlie as I am with Max," I said aloud. *Ha!*

I couldn't see *that* happening. Last week Charlie had asked if he could borrow a pen from me at the beginning of English class. I had handed him the pen wordlessly, positive that if I uttered even one word, my head would explode. His gorgeous smile had practically blinded me.

For half of the class I had practiced what I would say when Charlie gave the pen back. *Keep it,* I would tell him. *And think of me every time you flick your Bic.* But when the moment arrived, I was struck dumb yet again.

"Uh . . . keep it," I had mumbled finally. "I don't like that pen anyway. I mean, I like it. . . . I wouldn't have given you a bad pen. But I'm kind of tired of it. . . ." In two seconds I had gone from mute to bumbling idiot.

Charlie hadn't responded directly to my mumbles. But he *had* given me another warm smile. And possibly a wink. I still hadn't decided whether the movement I sensed in his eye was a twitch or a wink. Either way, he had given me back the pen—but with a heartfelt "thank you." Not a "thank you, *Jane,*" but still, it was something.

I sighed deeply. Charlie's face was burned into my brain. That face . . . that body . . . that warm laugh. *If only he would notice me, really notice me . . .* I was one hundred percent sure that if he gave me even half a chance, he would like me. We were definitely meant to be together—just not necessarily in this lifetime.

I was so deep into my detailed analysis of my five-second exchange with Charlie that I didn't notice at first that the phone was ringing. At about the fourth ring the vision of Charlie's face evaporated and I tuned back into reality.

I picked up the receiver of my Mickey Mouse phone (probably the least-hip telephone ever manufactured). "Hello?"

"Hey, girl," Nicole greeted me. "It's me."

"Actually, it's *us*," Christy added. "But you've got to speak up because Nicole is hogging the receiver."

"Hi, guys." I turned down my stereo and flopped onto my bed. "What's up?"

I could picture the two of them in Nicole's bedroom, having a mini tug-of-war as they both tried to listen to the conversation. I could also imagine the exchange that precipitated this phone call in the first place. If my instincts were correct, my best friends were about to grill me on my whereabouts this afternoon.

"We want to know what's up with *you*," Nicole declared, right on schedule. "Christy and I spent most of the afternoon speculating about this mysterious plan to snare the elusive Charlie Simpson."

I laughed. Nicole has a flair for the dramatic—probably because she faithfully records her favorite soap operas every day for later viewing. Part of me was dying to open my mouth and pour out every detail of my afternoon with Max. I knew my friends would be fascinated by my project.

*But Max and I both made a pact to keep our*

*deal a secret,* I reminded myself. Aside from the avalanche of humiliation I could experience if the wrong people found out about my transformation project, Max and I both realized that the faculty at Union High wouldn't view my "helping" Max write his papers with much enthusiasm.

"I'm giving myself a total makeover," I informed my friends. Not exactly the truth, but not a lie either. "I'm going to do everything in my power to turn myself into the kind of girl that would make Charlie Simpson's tongue hang out of his mouth."

"Like, you're going to start wearing eyeliner and lip gloss?" Christy asked. "And maybe get your hair highlighted?"

"Yes, yes, and maybe," I responded to Christy's rapid-fire questions. "But this is about a lot more than a cosmetic overhaul. I'm going to create a whole new *image* for myself."

Nicole whistled. "Sounds like a pretty major undertaking, Jane. What was your inspiration?"

I hesitated. Nicole was, if anything, perceptive. I could sense in her voice that she didn't think I was giving them the whole story.

"I, uh, found an article in a magazine about how to 'snag your crush,'" I told my friends. "I'm going to follow the steps and see if I get anywhere with you-know-who."

"What magazine?" Nicole asked.

"It was in . . ." Darn. I didn't want to tell an outright lie. But telling the outright truth wasn't an option either.

At that moment the doorbell rang downstairs. It was probably just an enterprising encyclopedia salesman, but said salesman couldn't have arrived at a better time. "Gotta go, guys," I said quickly. "There's an ax murderer at the door."

I hung up the phone and trotted downstairs. Since Mom and Dad were at their bimonthly potluck-dinner-slash-book-club night, I peeked through the curtains before I went to the door.

"Max!" I exclaimed.

I couldn't have been more surprised to see somebody if Ed McMahon himself had been standing on our front stoop with a Publisher's Clearing House check in his hand. And I immediately expected the worst.

I bolted to the front door and threw it open. "Hey, what's going on?" I asked. "Is there a problem? Did someone find out about our deal? Are you calling it off?"

Max took off the white baseball cap he was wearing and waved it in the air. "Truce! Truce!" he called. "Please, counsel, stop badgering the witness."

I giggled, stepping away from the door to let him inside. "Sorry . . . I guess I got a little nervous when I saw you standing out there."

Max laughed. "So much for relaxed and casual. I think we're going to have to do today's lesson all over again."

Oops. The guy had a point. I had totally blown my first opportunity to practice my new modus operandi.

"Let's start over," I suggested. Pause. "Hi, Max. How's it going?"

He grinned. "It's going great. What are you up to, Jane?"

I still wasn't sure what he was doing here, but this was definitely great "cool" practice. I shrugged nonchalantly. "I'm studying—suddenly I find myself with a lot more homework than usual."

He raised his eyebrows. "What *else* are you up to?"

Uh . . . I had no idea where he was going with this. "Let's see. . . . Well, I also have my stereo on," I informed him. "So I guess I'm listening to music."

"Much better," Max approved. "See, you're listening to music and doing a little homework."

I was getting more confused by the second. "Yeah, that's what I just said. I'm studying." Was there an echo in the living room?

Max shook his head in a way that was quickly becoming very familiar to me. "Jane, if a popular girl is home to answer the door, she'll never announce that she's spent the evening up in her room with her nose in the books."

"What does she say?" I asked. I resisted the urge to start pacing, realizing right away that walking back and forth across the living-room carpet wasn't the best way to project "relaxed."

"She'll tell you that she's giving herself a pedicure, listening to a new CD, talking to a friend on the phone," he explained. "And then, like an afterthought, she might say, 'And I'm doing a few of those trig problems.'"

"Oh." I felt stupid. And boring. I *never* polished my toenails. "I just study all the time." I sank onto our worn sofa and stuck a pillow over my head.

I felt Max sit down beside me. A moment later he plucked the pillow away from my eyes.

"You can still study, Jane," he assured me with a gentle smile. "Just call it something else—if anyone ever asks."

"Okay. I'll make a mental note." *I'll make a mental note to declare myself insane for thinking I could ever fit in with the popular crowd.*

"Now, what kind of music were you listening to as you painted your fingernails and gave yourself a new hairdo?" Max asked.

I sensed this was a test. And I was pretty sure I was going to fail. "Um . . . an opera," I confessed. "My dad has gotten really into opera lately, and I guess it, like, rubbed off on me."

Even *I* knew that opera wasn't cool. But since I didn't know what music *was* cool, I had no tools for lying to Max at my immediate disposal.

Predictably Max gave me his patented head shake. "No, no, no. Opera is no good." He paused. "I'll tell you what. Pick me up for school tomorrow morning. I'll give you a list of cool bands and bring along some tapes to play for the ride."

"It's a deal," I told him. Then I realized I still had no idea why Max had gone out of his way to come over here and quiz me on my evening. "Why are you here anyway?" I asked.

He grinned. "I wanted to check up on my favorite

pupil. Something told me this surprise visit would be a great opportunity for learning."

Suddenly I felt exponentially better than I had five minutes ago. If Max thought I was a lost cause, there was no way he would be wasting his time like this. Obviously he thought I had potential.

*I just need to realize that potential,* I thought. And now that I had Max, there was hope. Jeez. It was no surprise that I was known as Plain Jane Smith. Up until now I had been doing everything wrong.

*But that's going to change!* I promised myself. *As of right now.*

# Five

## Max

I WAS STILL stuffing tapes into my backpack when I heard Jane honking for me on Tuesday morning. I glanced at the digital clock on my nightstand and smiled. Jane was five minutes early—exactly as I should have known she would be.

I raced downstairs and ran out of the house. Jane was trusting me with her image—I didn't want to blow my own image by seeming like a lazy slob who couldn't get out of the house in the morning.

"Morning," I greeted Jane, sliding into the front seat of her VW Bug.

"Hey, Professor," she said with a big smile. "I can't wait for this morning's lecture."

I watched Jane as she revved the engine. It was funny. Until I was sitting across from her at Jon's Pizza the day before, I had never noticed how pretty she was. I mean, I had talked to Jane dozens of times over the years about tests and papers and homework assignments.

But I had never really *looked* at her. I had never noticed how her blue eyes sparkled when she was excited. And I had never realized that her blond hair was sort of a honey color. *Probably because she's always got it pulled back in a ponytail,* I added to myself.

Even now, at eight o'clock in the morning, Jane looked as fresh as . . . well, as fresh as a daisy. Her smooth skin glowed with a sort of natural light. And even though she wasn't wearing any makeup, Jane's lips were a deep, rosy red. *She's got the kind of prettiness that the experts are always calling "natural,"* I realized.

Shana looked totally gorgeous all the time. But she wore a ton of makeup to come off looking as natural as Jane! And I knew that for a fact. Her purse was usually loaded down with half a dozen of those little compacts. How many times had I given her a hug—and then discovered a virtual painter's palette on my crisp white T-shirt? Plus if I ever arrived early to pick her up for a date, Shana would stay in her room for an extra fifteen minutes, perfecting her hair and makeup.

Jane put the VW in gear, and the little car shot down the road. "I'm waiting, Professor," she told me. "Every second you're not talking, I'm not learning." She turned to me and shot me a warm grin.

I grinned back. Every time Jane gave me one of those dazzling smiles, I felt like laughing. She radiated vibrancy and passion and excitement—especially for this so-called project.

I still thought the whole endeavor was pretty weird, but I couldn't help being drawn in by Jane's enthusiasm. I was really trying to understand why getting noticed by the popular crowd was so important to her . . . but so far I hadn't been able to see why the lives of the "in" crowd were so much better than Jane's.

I picked up a shoe box full of tapes that was on the passenger-side floor of the Bug. Pavarotti. Mozart. Puccini.

"Jane, I hate to break it to you, but you've got a shoe box full of nerd music." I waved the box under her nose to emphasize my point. "Classical and opera are *not* the kinds of music that makes guys crazy."

Jane frowned. "But I *like* that music. Listening to a whole opera is an *experience*. The music is so dramatic and emotional. . . . It carries me away."

I shook my head. Wow. I could see that I was really going to have to work on Jane if I wanted her musical tastes to evolve into the twentieth century. I selected a tape labeled *La Bohème* and popped it into the car stereo. I planned to explain as we listened to the music why it belonged under the subheading Dullsville.

The music started, filling the car with what sounded like a hundred-piece orchestra. I glanced over at Jane. Her gaze was fixed on the road, but I saw a faraway look in her eyes. It was almost as if the opera music had transported her to a whole other world.

"Jane, you're spacing out on me," I said, nudging her arm.

"Let's just wait one minute. There's a great section coming up. A climactic scene in the opera."

"One minute," I agreed.

Leaning my head against the back of the black vinyl seat, I let my eyes drift shut. I had to admit that there was something pretty far-out about this music. The woman singing sounded like her guts were being ripped straight out of her body. It was heart wrenching!

"What's happening?" I asked Jane. "Is someone murdering her?"

Jane reached over and patted me on the shoulder. "Don't worry, Max. She's not dying—yet." She shifted the car into neutral, and we coasted to a stop in front of a red light. "Right now she thinks she's never going to see her lover again."

"Heavy." I knew that we had been listening to the opera for a lot more than a minute, but Jane seemed so entranced that I didn't have the heart to eject the tape so that we could get to the cool music.

Besides, I was kind of interested in hearing what was going to happen next. If the diva sounded like a wounded cow (a wounded cow with an amazing voice, of course), what was she going to pull out from her vocal cords when things got worse? I closed my eyes and listened.

"We're here." It seemed like only a second had passed when Jane's gentle voice interrupted the sound of the music.

"But . . . what happened?" I asked, opening my eyes and blinking several times into the light coming in through the windshield.

Jane grinned, then popped out the tape. "I'll tell you what. Why don't you borrow this? You can listen to the whole thing tonight."

I frowned. "I still won't know what happened," I pointed out. "They're all singing in, like, Italian. Or French. Or something."

"Italian," Jane informed me with a laugh. "And don't worry about understanding the words. Listen to the *music.*"

I took the tape from Jane's outstretched hand, slightly agog at the fact that I was volunteering to listen to an opera. *If anybody finds out about this, I'll be laughed off the baseball team,* I thought wryly.

But I was intrigued. Not only by the music, but by Jane's obvious knowledge of a subject so foreign to high schoolers across America. *But I'm supposed to be the teacher,* I reminded myself as Jane switched off the ignition.

"Hey, take this list of hip bands," I said, holding out the carefully typed list I had made last night. "And you'd better borrow a few of my tapes. From now on you can listen to *these* on the way to school."

I unzipped my backpack and pulled out a few tapes. I was sorry I wasn't going to get to see the expression on Jane's face as she listened to actual teenager music for maybe the first time ever.

Jane transferred the tapes to her overflowing shoe box. "I'll listen to them tonight," she promised.

"While I'm talking on the phone and perfecting my do-it-yourself manicuring techniques."

"And the homework?" I asked.

She shrugged, flipping her ponytail over one shoulder. "Oh, I don't know. . . . Maybe I'll try to get in a little reading for Atkison's class."

I felt like giving my A student a rousing cheer. "Good job, Jane. I think you're getting the hang of this stuff."

"I'd better be," Jane responded. "There are only a few more weeks of school, and I want to eradicate my geek status by graduation—if not sooner." She checked her watch. "Speaking of sooner, we'd better hurry. In two minutes we'll both be officially late to homeroom."

As I slid out of the car, I tried to identify the surge of emotion that was washing over me. And then I got it. A big ball of protectiveness had welled up inside me.

Jane was so sweet, and she was trying so hard. I hated the idea that people in school—some of them friends of mine—had made her feel invisible for the past four years. How could someone so adorable feel so undateable?

As we walked side by side toward the main building, both of us were quiet. I considered taking this opportunity to suggest to Jane that she didn't have to wear Levi's to school *every* day. But I decided against it. There would be plenty of time for constructive hints in the days to come.

*Really, it's too bad she wants to change,* I

mused. *Jane is quirky and interesting just the way she is.* I couldn't imagine that anyone who spent more than fifteen minutes talking to Jane Smith would call her "plain."

"See you later, Professor," Jane called out as we entered the building and headed to our separate homerooms.

*"Adiós,"* I called back. "That's Spanish."

I could still hear Jane's soft laughter in my mind when I opened the door to my homeroom. Then I realized I could hear something else. It was me. And I was humming a tune from *La Bohème.*

I laughed out loud. *Who is changing who?* I wondered.


"Where were you this morning?" Shana Stevens, my girlfriend, asked me as I sat down in the chair next to hers at our regular lunch table. "I waited by your locker, but you never showed up."

I slipped my arm around Shana's shoulders and squeezed her tight. "I got really into this album I was listening to," I explained (which was more or less the truth). "By the time I got to school, I had to go straight to homeroom."

"Well, I missed you." Shana turned toward me and leaned in close.

I inhaled the clean scent of her shampoo as I bent my head and touched her lips with mine. As always, I tasted Shana's lipstick as I kissed her. *Just once I would like to lock lips with my girlfriend and not feel like I'm snacking on a cosmetics factory,* I thought.

46

"I missed you too," I murmured, giving her another squeeze. "You look beautiful today."

And she did. In a short black miniskirt and a skintight white T-shirt, Shana looked like she had stepped off the pages of a fashion magazine. Her long, shapely legs were smooth and tanned, the toenails peeking out from her platform sandals expertly polished. *Picture-perfect,* I thought. *That's my girlfriend.*

"Are you two going to make out or eat?" Rose McNeal asked from across the table.

"Eating. Now, there's an appetizing notion," I commented, staring at the hideous mess (supposedly macaroni 'n' cheese) that covered my plate.

"That's why I bring a salad from Anderson's Market every day for lunch," Shana reminded me. "I wouldn't touch the so-called food they serve in this cafeteria with a three-foot lacrosse stick."

"According to Max, there are a lot of things you won't touch with a three-foot lacrosse stick," Charlie Simpson joked.

Madison Embry scooped into her mouth a spoonful of the vanilla nonfat yogurt she brought every day. "All I know is that one plate of mac 'n' cheese has more fat grams than I want to consume in a month."

"If only the rest of the cretins that inhabit these hallowed halls would join us in a revolt," Shana said. "Then maybe we could convince the administration to start serving sushi and tofu."

"I wouldn't want to unite with certain Union High students for *any* cause," Rose countered. "We might catch their inherent lameness."

I stuck a fork into my fat-filled mac 'n' cheese and tuned out the girls' conversation. Every lunch hour followed basically the same pattern. We all sat down at our table. Charlie, Scott, and I discussed our plans for baseball practice, then lapsed into silence while the girls competed to see who could come up with the nastiest sidebar.

"Speaking of lame, check out the revenge of the nerdettes over there," Shana said to the group. Her gaze traveled disdainfully from Jane to her two friends. "They're studying those fashion magazines like they were cramming for one of their advanced-placement chemistry classes."

"It's so pathetic," Madison announced, as if she were the ultimate arbiter of what was and was not pathetic in this world. "I mean, they're drooling over photos of prom dresses like they were actually going to get the chance to *wear* one."

Usually I barely even registered the girls' constant barrage of criticism. But today I found myself unable to ignore them. Hearing Shana, Madison, and Rose put down Jane and her friends was making me feel slightly sick to my stomach.

*Then again, an objective opinion on Jane's looks might give me a better idea about how to direct her in this transformation process,* I reasoned. *This could be totally valuable.* Even if it was also totally annoying.

"I don't get it," I said, interrupting the insult parade. "Why are those particular girls losers?"

Shana stared at me as if I had just grown another

head. "I'll assume that's a rhetorical question," she declared.

I shook my head. "Seriously. I mean, they're all nice and attractive and smart. . . . So why don't they have it? Why are they social outcasts?"

Shana wrinkled her nose. "Attractive? Under what dictionary do those three stooges qualify as *attractive?*"

"I think someone messed with his lemonade," Rose commented. "Either that or it's time for Max to take a trip to the eye doctor."

"Please. Just take a look at their geeky, blah clothes," Shana told me. "Notice their stupid ponytails." She was really getting into it now. "They don't even know that any decent, self-respecting girl doesn't go out in public without makeup. Have they ever heard the word *attitude?*"

"They look like they came to the cafeteria straight from gym class!" Madison added. "Ugh."

I kept nodding as Shana, Madison, and Rose continued to list reasons why Jane and her friends were losers. But inside, I disagreed. Would a loser make me laugh every time I had a conversation with her? Would a loser be able to light up a dark pizza place with her bright smile?

Nonetheless, I knew that Shana knew of what she spoke. As one of the most popular girls in school, she had a full understanding of what made a girl special in the eyes of her peers.

"Are you saying that with different hair and new clothes, one of those girls could have your look?" I asked. "I mean, if it's all about ponytails and blush brushes, any one of them should be able to elevate herself to your status."

"*My* status?" Shana asked, shooting me a warning glance.

"Well, she would never be as beautiful as you are," I added quickly. "But do you think an average girl could, you know, make herself stand out with the right changes?"

Shana shrugged. "Theoretically—but it'll never happen. Not one of those girls has the slightest sense of style."

I shoved another bite of macaroni into my mouth, pondering Shana's words. At the very back of my mind I was starting to contemplate a slightly bizarre idea.

The truth was that I *knew* what attracted me, at least physically, to a girl—it was sitting right next to me, hand on my knee. But I had no idea how to go about making Jane look like Shana and her friends.

That kind of makeover was a challenge meant for a self-possessed, stylish girl. And Shana was nothing if not stylish.

*Yeah, right,* I thought. *I can just imagine asking Shana to give Jane some pointers on the subject.*

*Bad idea.*

# Six

## Jane

"OH, HI, CHARLIE," I chirped casually. "How's it hanging?" Scratch that. "How's it going?"

*It's going great, Jane,* I answered myself. *I'm totally psyched that you've decided to come out of your shell. I've wanted to ask you out for the past four years, but I was always too intimidated by your brains to start a conversation.*

"Hey, a girl can have a fantasy now and then," I told my reflection in the mirror that hung in our front hallway.

But I had done enough talking into mirrors lately. Tonight I was going to have a shot at real-life, person-to-person, flirtatious banter. And I was so nervous that my mouth felt as if it were filled with saltwater taffy.

I paced across the living room, trying to work off some of the excess energy that had been building up inside me ever since Max suggested we hang out tonight for another lesson. I felt like I had downed a double espresso and a pound of chocolate.

*Chill out, Jane,* I ordered myself. There was no reason to be so jittery. After all, it was just this morning that I had felt so free and easy with Max, lecturing him on opera as we drove to school.

Outside, a horn beeped twice. *He's here!* I raced to the kitchen and grabbed my keys and my backpack off the table.

"Bye, Mom! Bye, Dad!" I yelled up the stairs.

"Bye, honey! Have a good time," Mom called from her bedroom.

One of the advantages of being a chronic good girl was that my parents never badgered me with the Great Inquisition before I left the house. Since they knew there was zero chance I'd be brought home by a police officer, they trusted me to make my own decisions. Thank goodness! I was *not* anxious to announce to my parents that I was going out with a guy on a *non*date in order to improve my heretofore *non*existent flirting skills.

I ran out the front door, slamming it shut behind me. By the time I got to Max's car and opened the passenger-side door, I was breathless from my forty-five-second sprint.

"Hi!" I panted. "Let's go."

I smiled at Max, taking in his freshly scrubbed face and carefully combed hair. In jeans and a crisp white button-down shirt, my nondate was definitely looking adorable.

"Wrong, Jane. This is all wrong." He gave me the head shake. "But I have to admit that your enthusiasm *is* a refreshing change of pace."

"Wrong?" I echoed. "I've already done something wrong? I just got here!"

"The thing is, the type of girl you're aspiring to be would never fly out of the house as soon as a guy honked his horn. She would wait for the guy to come to the door."

"Then why did you honk?" I demanded. "Now I feel like an idiot."

"Don't worry about it, Jane," Max said in his most teacherlike voice. "This was just a little pop quiz—next time I'm sure you'll pass." He paused. "But just to make sure, let's do it again."

I suppressed a wave of humiliation as I got out of the car. *This is exactly the kind of detail I'm aiming to absorb,* I told myself. No need to be ashamed. Besides, I had learned in the past few days that the faster I forced myself to move on from my endless social gaffes, the faster I made real improvements.

I slipped into the house and shut the door behind me. Inhale. Exhale. Inhale. Exhale.

"I'm back, Mom and Dad," I yelled upstairs. "But I'll be leaving again in a minute."

My breathing had slowed to a normal rate. Several seconds passed. And by the time the doorbell rang a minute later, I was totally composed.

Answering the door at the exact moment the

bell sounded probably wasn't much cooler than barreling out of the house on hearing the honk of a horn. *One, one thousand. Two, two thousand.*

In my mind I fast-forwarded time three weeks. I imagined myself wearing a slinky black prom dress and five-inch heels. On this side of the door I took a deep breath, at peace with myself and the world. Then—still in my head—I slowly opened the door. And saw Charlie Simpson, my date to the senior prom, looking absolutely gorgeous in a black tuxedo. Of course, he held the most beautiful corsage I had ever seen in his outstretched hand. . . .

I was so involved in the fantasy that I was actually disappointed to open the door—for real—and see Max Ziff standing there.

"Good evening, Max," I greeted him. "How nice to see you."

"Hi, Jane," Max answered with a grin. "You're looking lovely tonight."

My disappointment was quickly replaced with a small thrill from the compliment. Sure, Max only said I looked pretty because he was playing a part. But it was still nice to hear.

And I understood now why Max had insisted that I go back inside to start our nondate the right way. Running out to the car, I had felt like Max's buddy, his pal. But now, looking at him on my front doorstep, I felt like . . . well, like a *girl*.

And I liked it. I liked it a lot.

★   ★   ★

"So we've established that we can't go to the mall. Or to Wednesday's Café. Or to any of the other places where I usually hang out." Max tapped his fingers on the steering wheel, then turned to me. "Any ideas?"

Max and I had been driving aimlessly for fifteen minutes. But we still hadn't decided on a destination. First Max had suggested we go to the mall. Unfortunately there was a high probability that a bunch of Max's crowd would *also* be at the mall. And a sighting of Max Ziff with Plain Jane Smith would definitely cause a stir. Ditto every other place Max had suggested.

Our goal for tonight was clear. I was supposed to practice being witty and fun yet incredibly desirable and cool. I was supposed to be open but retain an air of mystery. The task was daunting enough without the threat of being spied on by a bunch of overly critical, nosy jocks.

"We need to go someplace where none of your friends would venture," I reasoned. "A place where we can be free to work on my transformation without the slightest fear of anyone discovering that I'm ghostwriting two of your term papers."

"I know that's what we need. But I'm out of ideas—"

"Turn left!" I interrupted. "I just had a flash of brilliance."

Obediently Max switched on his blinker and turned left. "Tell me."

"We'll go to King Louie's bowling alley," I

announced. "Nicole and Christy and I go there all the time. It's a blast, and the only people we ever see there are bald middle-aged men."

Max looked skeptical. "Bowling?" He paused. "Well . . . we definitely won't run into any of my friends at King Louie's. But Jane, bowling isn't cool."

I shrugged. "Do you have a better idea?"

"Nope." Max pressed on the gas and sped toward Route 2, which led to the bowling alley. "I guess it's fine for tonight. As long as you realize that someone like Shana would *never* think that knocking down pins in rented shoes was a fun way to pass an evening."

"I'll hang up my bowling shirt after tonight," I promised.

Twenty minutes later I was attempting to show Max how to choose the right bowling ball. He hadn't been joking when he told me that he had never bowled before.

"How about this one?" Max asked, holding up a small, pink bowling ball for my inspection.

I giggled. "Uh, that would be the perfect ball—for an eighty-year-old lady." I picked up a large, black bowling ball and handed it to Max. "Try that one."

Max took the bowling ball in his right hand, flung back his arm, then lurched toward the lane. I watched as he dropped the ball with a thud. It rolled slowly toward the pins.

"Yes!" Max shouted. "I think it's gonna be a strike!"

The ball veered left and dropped into the gutter.

"Or not," I commented wryly. I picked up a ball for myself. "Watch and learn."

I held the ball in my right hand, balancing it with my left. Then I used my best bowling form to take three steps forward as I swung my right arm behind me. When I at last released the ball, it sped straight down the center of the lane. A moment later all ten pins clattered to the floor.

"Now, *that's* a strike!" I jumped up and down, and Max slapped me a high five.

"Wow!" he exclaimed. "That was, like, art."

I laughed. "It's not all that hard, Max. By the end of tonight I personally guarantee you'll get at least one strike."

"If I get a strike, will you buy me one of the embroidered polyester King Louie Lanes bowling shirts?" he asked, wiggling his eyebrows.

I groaned. "Even *I* know that a King Louie customized button-down isn't the fashion statement anyone in their right mind would make," I retorted. "But the shoes *are* pretty cool."

For a moment Max looked horrified. Then he laughed. "That was a joke. Right?"

I shrugged nonchalantly. "Maybe. Maybe not."

For the next hour I coached Max on the finer points of amateur bowling. I had never thought of myself as an athlete (and I still doubted that bowling qualified as an actual sport), but it felt good to be better than an established jock at *any* game involving a ball.

"Are we still keeping score?" Max asked finally.

"Unfortunately for you, yes," I answered. Glancing at the scorecard, I couldn't help but laugh. "You're up to fifty," I informed him. "I, on the other hand, have bowled one hundred and twenty so far."

Suddenly Max dropped to the floor and did ten push-ups. Around us, families turned to watch.

"Max, what are you doing?" I hissed. "Everybody is *looking* at you—and not in a good way."

He jumped up with a grin. "That's my good-luck ritual," Max explained. "I do ten push-ups before every baseball game—and right now I need all the help I can get." He turned and waved to the people who were watching. "Thanks, folks. The show's over!"

I wasn't sure whether I should be embarrassed or delighted. I wasn't used to drawing attention to myself, but part of me loved Max's carefree self-confidence. Not for the first time this evening, I realized I had never had such a good time with someone of the male persuasion.

*I've never had so much fun with anyone, for that matter.* Talk about bizarre! In a million years I wouldn't have guessed that I could feel so comfortable around a guy like Max.

"I'm having an extrasensory moment," I told Max. "I predict a strike in your very near future."

He held the bowling ball in both hands and gave it a big kiss. "From your mouth to the bowling gods' ears."

"Position!" I cried out. "Remember to position your feet!"

Max stood directly in front of the lane and stared at the pins for several seconds. Then he took three steps, just as I had shown him. At the same time he pulled his right arm back in a full, fluid motion. A moment later the ball rolled down the lane. . . .

"Strike!" I screamed. "Strike!" So much for not wanting to bring attention to myself.

"Yes!" Max shouted. "I did it!"

He sprinted toward me, then grabbed me in his arms and swung me around. "Strike!" I repeated.

I didn't know what else to say. For the first time in my life a guy other than my grandfather or father had swept me up in a spontaneous hug. It was a big event—even if the guy was Max.

He set me down. "Uh . . . sorry about that. I guess I got a little overexcited."

Great. My first hug, and he wished he could take it back. *Max is probably thinking about how stupid he would feel if any of his friends had seen that,* I thought.

"No problem," I told him.

He grinned. "What the heck . . ." He pulled me close again, squeezing me tight. "Thanks, Jane," Max said as he let me go. "I haven't felt this kind of adrenaline rush since I hit my first home run in Little League. Who knew bowling was such a blast?"

"I did," I pointed out. "It was *my* suggestion."

"Touché."

I glanced at my watch. Oops. It was getting pretty late, and so far Max and I hadn't worked on my witty/fun/flirtatious/mysterious/desirable lesson at all.

"We'd better get started on tonight's curriculum, Professor," I announced. "Can I buy you some nachos at the snack bar while you tutor me?"

Max gave me that you're-an-alien glance. Uh-oh. What had I messed up now? Were nachos inherently uncool? Was the mention of the words *snack* and *bar* the kiss of death?

"Jane, we've been conducting our lesson since we got here," he declared. "And you did very well, I'd like to add."

I was stunned. "But . . . but I was just being myself the whole time!" I exclaimed. "I didn't know it was a test!"

Max shrugged. "I guess this means you're a natural at being cool and fun, Jane Smith."

Now I was the one who wanted to throw *my* arms around Max. This had to feel ten times better than getting a strike. Max Ziff had just informed me that I had spent a whole evening in a mode he described as both "fun" and "cool." And I hadn't even been trying!

"We're really getting somewhere," I said excitedly. "Max, thank you so much!"

"You're welcome." He sat down and untied his bowling shoes. "Jane, I think we're done. Tonight proves that you're the kind of girl my friends would go for."

*Yeah, right!* I thought angrily. *I'm sure Charlie Simpson would jump at the chance to take me bowling!*

"That's nice of you to say," I replied, my voice icy. "But we both know it's not true."

"Jane—," Max started.

I held up one hand to stop him from continuing. Anything he said would just make it worse. "I don't look anything like Shana and her friends!" I cried, furious that I even had to humiliate myself by pointing out such an obvious (not to mention painful) fact. "If anything, you and your friends might deign to play a game of basketball with me or something."

"But that's not what I mean. . . ." His voice trailed off, and he gave me a sort of woeful puppy-dog stare.

"Are you getting bored of this whole project?" I blurted out. "Is that why you're trying to convince me that we're through?"

"No, Jane . . . I . . ." He stopped talking, then slipped off the bowling shoes and pushed his feet into his brown loafers. "Listen, we should probably get going."

"Yeah, we probably should." The enthusiasm had completely gone out of my voice as I spoke.

*I can't believe Max is letting me down.* If he had his way, Max's part of our bargain was finis. And I was still Plain Jane Smith. I was upset about the prospect of not completing my transformation.

But worse than that . . . I was disappointed in Max. And yes, I was hurt. So hurt that all I wanted to do was get home, crawl into bed, and cry.

# Seven

## Max

JANE HADN'T SAID more than two words since we left the bowling alley. I felt a tight knot in the pit of my stomach as I remembered the cold way she'd stared at me when I told her that I thought her metamorphosis was complete. She was the last person in the world I wanted to hurt . . . and yet I didn't know how to *help*.

"Well, we're here!" I said brightly as I pulled up in front of the Smiths' house. "Home, sweet home."

She didn't say anything. And she didn't make a move to get out of the car. *Good going, Ziff. You've made the girl so upset, she's catatonic.*

"Uh, Jane? We're here."

"I realize that," she said stiffly. "I'm waiting for you to get out and open my door for me. Isn't that what *Shana* would do?"

I smiled at Jane's valiant attempt to stay a step ahead of The Rules. "Actually, none of the girls do that—they just go ahead and get out."

"Oh, okay." Jane's face was so sad that I was afraid she about to burst into tears.

Once again I felt a huge wave of protectiveness toward my so-called pupil. The thought of Jane crying made me feel horrible. As she started to open the car door, I put my hand on her arm to stop her.

"Wait a second—we need to talk." Jane frowned, but she leaned back into her seat and looked at me, her eyes questioning. "I'm not bored with our project at all," I continued. "But I'm worried that I can't help you with all of the girlier stuff in your metamorphosis. I mean, what do I know about hair and makeup?"

"You know more than I do," Jane insisted. "I know zilch, zero, nada."

"The point is . . . You've made it clear tonight that what you want most of all is to look different."

"I won't argue with that thesis statement," Jane agreed in her typically quirky, endearing way. "Basically I want to *not* recognize myself in the mirror."

I stared at Jane's face, unable to comprehend why she would want to transform herself into someone else. "But you're so—"

"So *what?*" she snapped, interrupting me.

*Beautiful as it is,* I finished silently.

"So plain and ordinary that I couldn't look like Shana or her friends no matter what I tried?"

The girl had no confidence! If I hadn't witnessed her low self-esteem in the looks department myself, I would have thought she was faking this. And I knew Jane didn't play mind games.

"I was *about* to say, 'But you're so cute as is,'" I informed her.

Cute *is a better word than* beautiful, I told myself. *Beautiful* would have been . . . well, not entirely appropriate. Under the circumstances.

Jane smiled, but the smile didn't reach her eyes. "Thanks for the vote of confidence," she said softly. "But I know what I look like. And to prove how plain I am, I haven't had a single date all through high school."

"Jane . . ." Tears welled up in her eyes. She blinked them away, the small drops making her deep blue eyes even darker.

"All I've ever really wanted was to go to the prom," she admitted. "I wanted to go with someone I really liked so I could have just one incredible night of feeling special, pretty . . . wanted."

"Is that what this whole turn-Jane-into-a-popular-girl-look-alike project is all about?" I asked. "Are you doing this to get a date to the prom?"

She nodded, staring at her hands, which were folded in her lap. "I must sound pretty stupid," Jane commented, her voice barely above a whisper. "Now that I'm saying this stuff out loud . . . well, I don't know what I was thinking."

My heart ached for Jane. She was so sweet, so vulnerable, so *Jane*. I hated to hear her sound so defeated. Especially because I knew that she was dead wrong. Any guy would be lucky to have her as a date to his senior prom. With Jane the night would be one to remember.

*I can't let her down,* I realized. I had to find a way to help her. Period.

"First of all, you're not stupid," I said firmly. "I admire you. Not very many people have the guts to go after something they really want."

"Yeah, well . . . a lot of good it's done me." She clenched and unclenched her fists, then turned her head and looked straight into my eyes. "Thanks for everything you've done, Max. But I know when it's time to quit."

"Listen, I have an idea. A foolproof way to turn you into a glamour girl—practically overnight."

"You do?" Jane's eyes brightened.

I nodded. "Yep. But we'd have to include someone else in our project." I paused to let her absorb what I had said. "So . . . are you up for it?"

"I don't know—who's this other person?" Jane sounded wary but hopeful.

"I can't tell you yet," I responded. "But I promise that it's someone you can trust."

I held my breath as I waited for Jane to tell me whether or not she would go along with plan B. *Say yes,* I urged silently.

"Okay, I'll do it," she announced finally. "No guts, no glory."

Jane flashed me one of her dazzling smiles, and I instantly felt better. Somehow I had managed to salvage the evening after putting not only my foot but my fist as well into my mouth.

*Now all I have to do is set the plan into action,* I thought. And that might not be as easy as I hoped.

At seven o'clock the next morning I was sitting in my girlfriend's living room, gearing up for a possibly major begging session. If I knew Shana Stevens, the caffé latte and almond croissant I had brought along would go a long way toward putting her in the mood to say yes to the favor I was about to ask.

"Shana will be right down, Max," Mrs. Stevens told me. "But watch out for yourself. She's not at her sunniest this early in the morning."

I grinned. "Thanks, Mrs. Stevens."

A full five minutes later, Shana stomped into the living room. And she wasn't smiling.

"Max, what are you doing here?" she demanded. "I just woke up! I haven't even taken a shower, much less put on my makeup or curled my hair."

"Good morning to you too," I greeted her. Then I held out the breakfast I had brought. "A peace offering for dragging you into the public eye so early in the morning."

What was it with girls and hair? They seemed to think they weren't actual human beings until they had sprayed, curled, or teased.

Shana seemed to warm up to me as she peered into the bag. "Thank you, sweetie," she said. "I don't mean to be a jerk. . . . I just want to look good for you."

I took a couple of steps toward Shana and

enfolded her in my arms—caffé latte and almond croissant included. "You look gorgeous exactly the way you are."

And I meant it. I preferred to see Shana the way she looked now, without all of her carefully applied makeup. With her hair falling around her shoulders and her face fresh and clean, Shana was natural and soft . . . feminine.

*Like Jane.* The thought had come from out of nowhere. But it was true. Since I had been hanging out with Jane, I had been thinking about girls in a whole new way. Essentially I had discovered that girls were people too.

Shana and I had been going out for six months, and our relationship was solid. But had we really gotten to know each other yet? I loved her because she was beautiful, and because we were in the same crowd, and because we did all of the same things on weekends.

But those couldn't be the *only* reasons I loved Shana. There had to be more. Deep down, Shana and I obviously had some kind of connection. Right?

*Then again, I've never really thought about it before,* I mused. We got along; we were attracted to each other. . . . Until now it had seemed that those were the only important elements in a relationship.

"He*llooo?*" Shana snapped her fingers in front of my nose. "Max? Are you in there?"

I blinked. "I was thinking about how lucky I am to have you for a girlfriend," I said, which was sort of true. "Now, what did you ask me?"

Shana gave me a smile and fluffed her hair. "I wanted to know why you felt it necessary to come over here so early."

Ah, yes. Back to the issue at hand. Turning Jane into an "it" girl. I clasped Shana's hand and led her to the Stevens's overstuffed, floral-print sofa. She sat down and looked at me skeptically.

"Is this bad news?" she asked. "Because I don't deal with bad news before eleven o'clock."

"No bad news," I assured her. "Actually, I want to ask you for a favor. It's going to sound pretty strange at first—but it's important to me."

Shana raised an eyebrow. "Go on."

"You know Jane Smith, right?" I asked. I realized that I was standing in front of Shana, sort of looming over her. Quickly I sat down beside her.

"Plain Jane Smith," Shana responded, her voice laced with contempt. "What about her?"

My jaw tightened slightly at Shana's dismissive acknowledgment of Jane. But I forced myself to smile pleasantly.

I cleared my throat, feeling more nervous by the second at the prospect of revealing the bargain that Jane and I had made to Shana. "She's helping me out with something," I explained. "And in return, I'm helping *her* out."

"I don't get it." Shana sipped her caffé latte and gave me a blank stare.

"I'm really busy right now," I said, circling around the issue. "And I have these two huge term papers to write."

"Uh-huh . . ." Shana sounded bored. She was probably irritated that this conversation was cutting into her primping time.

I had to cut to the heart of the matter. "Basically, Jane Smith is writing my term papers for me," I told Shana. "And in exchange, I'm helping her transform herself."

"Transform herself? What does that mean?"

"Jane wants to fit in with our crowd," I explained. "She wants to be like you and Rose and Madison. . . . You know, the kind of girl that guys really go for."

"You've got to be joking," Shana declared. "Plain Jane couldn't be like me and my friends if she spent the rest of her *life* trying. The raw material simply isn't there."

Not the response I was hoping for. But I wasn't exactly shocked that Shana's initial reaction was so negative. She had offered more or less the same opinion about Jane's potential when I had brought it up indirectly at lunch yesterday.

"If you really *look* at Jane, you'll see that she does have what it takes," I insisted. "I mean, she's got pretty blue eyes, a great smile, and totally smooth skin." I envisioned Jane as I spoke, remembering the way that smile had filled me with warmth when we were bowling last night. "And her hair—"

"I get the picture," Shana interrupted. "Although you're the *only* one who can see it—Plain Jane Smith is, in reality, Kate Moss in hiding."

Oops. I had been waxing a little too poetic about another girl. And it didn't help that the girl in question was someone that Shana thought was on the bottom of the high-school-cliques food chain.

But it was hard *not* to say great things about Jane. In the past few days I had discovered that Jane was the kind of person *I* would like to be. Open. Honest. Smart. Brave. *But Shana doesn't need to know all of that,* I reasoned. *Once she gets to know Jane, she'll see those qualities herself.* Hopefully.

All of these thoughts came one after the other, overlapping and mixing in my brain. Only a second had passed when I spoke.

"Obviously Jane can never be as beautiful as you are," I told Shana. "And you're ten times more interesting and dynamic than Jane is."

*But I don't believe that,* I thought. *It's a lie.* Jane was different from Shana—but she wasn't *less*. In her own unique way Jane was simply awesome. Still, the words seemed to have a soothing effect on Shana. Her face brightened.

"Can't we help her out?" I asked, not letting the question die. "Think about how good you would feel if you made another girl realize her potential."

Shana sighed. "Okay. I'll do it."

I knew I was beaming as I put my arms around Shana and hugged her tight. "Thank you, thank you, thank you."

"You're welcome," she responded. "But don't expect any miracles."

I grinned. Jane didn't *need* a miracle. All she needed were a few fashion tips and some makeup lessons. I couldn't wait to tell her the good news.

# Eight

## Jane

*I* *HOPE I won't regret this,* I thought as I slammed the door of my locker shut on Wednesday afternoon. Max had promised we were going to begin the most important part of my metamorphosis today. I was to turn from caterpillar into butterfly with the help of the right clothes, the right hair, and the right makeup.

But I still didn't know the identity of the mystery person Max had enlisted to help us. Which was why my heart was pounding so hard in my chest.

I strode down the corridor, attempting to have that I'm-cool-and-confident-don't-mess-with-me air. I hesitated when I saw that Shana was standing next to Max at his locker. As comfortable as I felt around Max, I still didn't have the nerve to approach him when Shana Stevens was within a five-classroom vicinity.

Max caught sight of me. "Jane, over here!" he called.

So much for avoiding Miss Popularity. I ambled toward the happy couple, mentally preparing myself for a painfully awkward exchange of pleasantries.

"Hey, Max," I greeted him.

He gave me a warm, encouraging smile. "Jane, do you know my girlfriend, Shana?"

I nodded. "Hi, Shana." Okay, so we didn't officially *know* each other. But I knew who she was.

"Hello, Jane." Shana smiled in a friendly way, but I couldn't help but notice that she was appraising me from head to toe with her icy blue eyes.

I felt about two feet tall as I glanced toward Max. *What's the deal?* I asked silently.

Max seemed to read my mind. "Shana is the person who is going to lead you down the glamour path," he explained. "I've filled her in on what we've been doing, and she's totally psyched to help out."

I gulped. Shana Stevens, the most popular girl in school, was going to take time out of her busy social life for *me?* It seemed impossible. But here she was, nodding while Max informed me of this new development. *Who did you think he was going to enlist for the project?* I asked myself. *Tyra Banks?*

"Thanks, Shana," I said softly. "I really appreciate it."

She shrugged. "Don't worry about it. One trip to the mall and I'll have you looking like . . . well, looking a whole lot better." She paused. "No offense."

"Great!" Max clapped. "Ladies, let's proceed to

the parking lot. Your chariot—or at least my parents' Saturn—awaits."

I laughed at Max's joke, but Shana merely rolled her eyes. As I followed Max and Shana down the hall, I was all too aware that my gait was neither cool nor confident. But I was willing to endure a few hours of discomfort if it meant getting Shana's expert advice.

Who knew? Maybe by the end of the afternoon Shana would realize that I had a lot more to offer than she ever could have guessed. After all, Max seemed to like me. Was it such a crazy notion that his girlfriend could like me too?

I thought of the many times I had seen Shana and her friends sneering at me. Not once had any of them picked me for a team in gym class or offered me a seat in the cafeteria. For that matter, in four years none of them had ever addressed me in an even semicordial manner.

*But they were reacting to the old Plain Jane Smith*, I reminded myself. The remodeled version of me might be just the kind of girl that Shana would want to hang out with on a Friday night. . . .

"We're definitely going to have to do something about her clothes," I heard Shana say to Max. "She looks like she robbed an army-supply store."

. . . Okay, so maybe it was going to take some time for Shana to see that there was a cool person behind this baggy shirt and these faded jeans. *I'll just hope for the best,* I decided. *And expect the worst!*

★   ★   ★

"The fifteen square feet surrounding us should be every young woman's Mecca," Shana informed me twenty minutes later.

As soon as we had entered the mall, Max had left us (abandoned us, in my opinion) in order to participate in an air-hockey tournament at the arcade with his baseball teammates. Think of Shana as your fairy godmother, Max had told me.

I *had* been wishing for exactly that. A fairy godmother, complete with delicate wings and glitter-dusted hair. But in my mind, my Glinda the Good Witch was slightly less intimidating. As friendly as I could tell Shana was trying to be, she obviously wasn't used to conversing with someone of my social nonstanding.

We stood in front of the Lancôme counter in Macy's cosmetic department, where I was faced with an overwhelming display of eye shadows, lipsticks, powders, blushes, perfumes, and creams. I had walked by similar displays dozens of times in the past, but I had never really absorbed the sheer number of products that a girl could use to "enhance" her so-called natural beauty. As far as I could tell, there was nothing *natural* about it.

"Are you armed to charge?" Shana asked, spritzing herself with something she had referred to as "body mist."

"Uh . . . what?" I had noticed that Shana, unlike Max, spoke in a particular lingo that I was finding difficult to decode.

"A credit card. Do you have a credit card?" She

grabbed another of the tiny, pastel-colored sample bottles and held it to her nose.

"Oh yeah. I mean, yes, I have a credit card."

Thanks to years of responsible baby-sitting, I was one of the few teenagers in America who had my own (not my parents') credit card. Up until now I had barely used it. But I had a feeling that was about to change—in a very expensive way.

"Good. You're going to need it," Shana responded. "If you want to look like the kind of girl that Max and his friends would go for, you want to look like me and my friends, right?"

I nodded. "Yes, definitely."

"Well, a little pink lip gloss isn't enough," she informed me. "You're going to need a *total* makeup makeover."

"Whatever you say, Shana. I'm in your hands."

She turned to the saleswoman. "Consider the girl's face a blank canvas," she said to the lady. "She needs a new look, from moisturizer to lip liner."

The petite woman's face lit up. "Yes, of course. We'll bring out the cheekbones . . . and contour the lines around her nose. And then we'll give her eyebrows an actual *shape*."

Shana was nodding vigorously. "She needs major plucking. Right now she's more or less sporting a unibrow."

I tried to follow the rapid-fire conversation between the saleswoman and Shana, but they were speaking in what sounded like a foreign language. Somewhere between the mention of under-eye concealer and eyelash curlers, I decided I'd sit back and let the experts try to make me pretty—by any means necessary.

For a full thirty minutes the saleswoman, who introduced herself as Tiffany (Tiff, for short), worked on my face. As she brushed, blushed, and lipsticked, I listened to her endless, instructive monologue. Not for the first time during my entire transformation process, I wished Max hadn't banned my notebook.

"Don't worry, Jane," Shana said. "We'll buy you a copy of *Cindy Crawford's Basic Face* so you can practice doing all of this stuff on your own."

Apparently my face was an easy read. I wondered if Shana could also read the anticipation that was building up inside me. Tiffany kept murmuring about my "splendid cheekbones" and "ripe lips." I was starting to believe that with enough pounds of powder on my face, there was actual hope for me.

At last Tiffany set down her eyebrow pencil and sighed contentedly. "Voilà!" she exclaimed. "I have created a masterpiece."

"You look great, Jane," Shana said, her voice warmer than it had been all afternoon.

I was almost afraid to look when Tiffany handed me a small mirror to hold up to my face. What if I had purple eye shadow up to my hairline? Or bright pink lipstick that made me look like a relative of one of the Teletubbies?

I lifted the mirror and gazed into my brand-new reflection. "Wow . . ."

The person staring back at me bore a faint

resemblance to Plain Jane Smith. But we were distant cousins, at most. My usually boring blue eyes practically popped out of my head, and I could actually *see* those cheekbones that Tiffany had kept commenting on. Even my skin looked different. . . . It sort of glowed from within.

Sure, I was wearing the same old pair of jeans and blah shirt. But my face—my face looked like the kind of face that went on dates and ate lunch at the popular table and laughed in the hallways at school with good-looking guys. The uncool clothes and dorky ponytail still needed to go. But hey, one step at a time—I was making progress. Amazing, unbelievable, awe-inspiring progress.

"Thanks, Shana." I hopped off the high stool I was sitting on, and before I could think twice, I threw my arms around her. "This is so great of you."

Shana patted me on the back. "Don't worry about it."

As Tiffany happily began to ring up my dozen purchases, I stared at Shana, who was applying a shade of deep rose lipstick. She still looked like the ultimate ice queen, with her nose stuck in the air, every hair in place, and her designer clothes. But clearly she was a lot more than a seventeen-year-old fashion plate. She had done me an enormous favor.

"Why are you doing this?" I asked, unable to help myself.

Shana blotted her lips with a Kleenex, contemplating the question. "Well, it's always struck me as a waste when girls walk around looking horrendous when they could look good if they tried." She smiled. "No offense."

Huh. I knew I hadn't exactly been a model look-alike before now, but I had never thought of myself as *horrendous*. Frankenstein's monster was horrendous. I was merely plain and ordinary and nothing to notice in a crowded room.

But I wasn't about to point out all of that to Shana. What was the saying? *Don't look a gift horse in the mouth.* Shana had helped me out, and I was grateful. That was the important thing.

Shana glanced at the slim gold watch that encircled her slim, perfect wrist. "We'd better get going," she announced. "Max promised to take me out to dinner in exchange for . . . uh, well, he promised to take me out to dinner."

I signed the receipt Tiffany handed me without allowing myself to fully comprehend the amount I had just spent on cosmetic products. I would have to log dozens of hours with the Moellers' toddler to pay for my brand-new face. But if I got a date with Charlie Simpson, every minute spent splashing in the kiddie pool would be well worth it.

As I followed Shana out of the department store, I kept turning my head to glance at myself in the endless row of mirrors. Each time I was surprised to see the face that gazed back at me. I couldn't wait to see Max's face. Would he believe that the girl who'd introduced him to the joys of opera and bowling could be the same girl who he was about to meet?

"There he is," Shana announced as we left the

store and headed toward the mall's enormous food court. Max was standing, as instructed, next to the giant, neon, first-floor map of the mall.

"If Max has eaten an order of chili fries, I'm going to kill him," Shana continued. "I don't want to be the only one at dinner who's hungry—I'll have to get by on a small dinner salad and a couple of rolls."

I wasn't quite grasping the connection between an order of chili fries and Max and Shana's romantic dinner (I assumed it had something to do with a girly girl not eating more than her boyfriend at mealtime), but at the moment I didn't care. More pressing concerns were consuming the sum total of my brainpower. Such as . . . how was Max going to respond to my makeover?

"Drumroll, please!" Shana cried when we were within earshot of Max. "I present Jane—my newest creation!"

*Actually, I'm Tiffany's creation,* I thought. But so what? I took a deep breath and stared at Max, waiting for a reaction.

At first he just blinked. Then his mouth dropped open just a little and his eyebrows went up into his forehead. "Whoa . . ."

"What do you think?" I asked, my voice cracking. *Please say I look great. Or even good. Or even fine.*

"You look amazing," Max said slowly, as if he still wasn't sure he was looking at the same Plain Jane Smith he had sent off to the makeup counter with Shana a little less than an hour ago. "Truly . . . amazing."

I gulped. "Thanks." I absorbed Max's compliment,

79

his words echoing over and over in my mind.

My knees began to feel wobbly. In a Jane Austen novel I would have been described as about to "swoon." Sure, Max had said nice things to me before. But this was something new. His eyes were locked to my face, staring, staring, staring.

"Let's go, Max," Shana announced, her voice slightly shrill. "I made reservations at Café Bouche." She turned to me. "You can get back to your car from here, right, Jane?"

"Yes, of course," I answered automatically. Shana's tone didn't leave much room for argument.

Besides, I wasn't ready to leave the mall yet. I hadn't been poring over *Vogue* and *Elle* for the past week for no reason. I had every intention of going on a minor shopping spree.

"Are you sure?" Max asked. He glanced at Shana, then back at me.

"Yes!" I insisted. "Go!"

As I watched Max take Shana's hand and lead her toward the escalator, I felt an annoying pang of envy. It wasn't that I was jealous of Shana and Max per se. But I wished *I* were the one heading off to a romantic, candlelit dinner with a great guy.

*Don't despair,* I commanded myself. The look in Max's eyes had assured me that yes, I was turning into the kind of girl Max and his friends would go for.

*I have the look now, and I've had the lessons in how to act,* I reminded myself. *Now all I've got to do is find a way to make Charlie Simpson notice!*

★   ★   ★

"Don't just sit there!" I begged Nicole and Christy a couple of hours later. "Tell me if you like it!"

I was standing in the Gilmores' basement, blocking my two best friends' view of the television set. Every Wednesday night, in what had become something of a sacred ritual, they got together for their own must-see TV. (I usually stayed away since when I watched television I spent most of the time pointing out stupid dialogue and wondering how anyone ever sat through the commercials.)

But I couldn't contain my excitement about my new look, and I had burst into Nicole's house to show off my makeover for my small (but intensely supportive) fan club. Both Nicole and Christy appeared to be speechless—a rare event that I took as a good sign.

"You look awesome!" Nicole finally exclaimed. "But . . . what happened?"

"Did you go on one of Oprah Winfrey's makeover shows without telling us?" Christy asked. "Or did you get all of this from a magazine?"

"Max did it!" I burst out. I couldn't keep my secret from my friends a moment longer. "Actually, Tiffany, the cosmetics saleswoman, did it. But it's all because of Max."

Nicole pushed the mute button on her remote control. "Max? As in Max Ziff? How did he get involved in your self-improvement plan?"

Christy grinned. "Are you and Max . . . you know . . . an item?"

I shook my head vigorously. "Of course not!

81

He's totally in love with Shana." I paused, unsure of how to explain our deal without breaking my promise to Max that I wouldn't tell anyone I was writing his term papers.

"Don't stall!" Nicole insisted. "We want to know everything!"

At last I took a deep breath. Then in the most vague terms possible I explained to my friends that Max and I had agreed to trade favors.

"And as his favor to me, Max is helping me become the type of girl he and his friends would go for," I finished.

"In other words, the kind of girl that Charlie Simpson would ask to the prom," Christy commented.

I felt myself blushing, but I nodded. "Exactly."

"Well, all I can say is that Tiffany-the-blush-girl really knows her stuff," Nicole declared. "You look like a cover girl."

Talk about magic words! I basked in Nicole's compliment as if I had just been crowned Miss America. Shallow? Yes. But I had spent the past four years being deep and thoughtful. Right now all I wanted was to be hip and pretty.

"I can't wait to try out the new me at school tomorrow," I said with a sigh. "I just hope Max's reaction is everything I'm hoping it will be."

Christy frowned. "Max? Uh, don't you mean *Charlie?*"

I nodded. "Right. I mean, Charlie." I paused, flustered. "Did I say 'Max'?"

"You said 'Max,'" Nicole confirmed.

That was weird. I had been thinking about Charlie, but Max's name had accidentally slipped out.

"Anyway, I can't wait to get to school tomorrow," I said cheerfully.

"Jane, you do look great," Christy said, her voice a bit too tentative for my liking. "But don't you think the Cindy Crawford makeup job might be a little much for everyday wear?"

I shrugged. "You're just not used to it," I responded confidently.

It took time for people to adjust to a new look. And I had no doubt that within a week, Nicole and Christy would be as enthusiastic as I was. Besides, as much as I loved my friends, they weren't my target audience. Charlie was.

# Nine

## Jane

"MIND IF I sit down?" a soft voice whispered in my ear the next afternoon.

Despite the fact that he was whispering, I recognized Max's voice immediately. "Sure," I whispered back, glancing away from the pile of notes in front of me to give him a smile.

It was the last period of the day, and I had retreated to the library to take full advantage of my Thursday-afternoon study hall.

Max slid into a chair and placed a book on the table. "It's about John Kennedy," he informed me, pointing to the book.

I gestured toward a stack of books—all about President Kennedy—at the end of the table. I had checked them out in order to research Max's history paper. "I think I'm covered," I told him.

He nodded. "Just the same, I want to help you out. What if the teacher grills me about my paper? I'd better be ready to answer questions."

I handed him a neat stack of blank index cards. "In that case, I would be much obliged if you'd start writing down relevant quotes."

Hey, working on his paper—even the research part—wasn't something Max had to do according to the terms of our agreement. But I wasn't about to say so. Between my personal mission and the awe-inspiring number of pages I had to write before the end of the semester, I was in way over my head.

After a few minutes I almost forgot that Max was sitting beside me, carefully copying quotes about JFK onto my note cards. We worked silently, totally absorbed in our research. I had never felt so comfortable with a guy that I could be just inches away from him yet not be totally self-conscious.

Finally I set down my pen and shook out a cramp in my hand. "Wow, it's almost last bell," I commented, catching sight of my watch.

Max looked up from his textbook. "Hooray." He shut the book and leaned back in his chair. "By the way . . . I, uh, like what you've done with your new look. I mean, you know, going kind of lighter on the makeup."

"Um . . . thank you." I don't know why we both seemed tongue-tied all of a sudden. Maybe because members of the opposite sex didn't usually sit around a library table gabbing about rouge.

"I mean, you looked awesome yesterday.

Really glamorous. But it was sort of over the top." He paused. "That didn't come out right. What I meant to say is that you don't need a lot of makeup to look great."

Max was right. I was wearing a lot less makeup than I had been immediately post-Tiffany. But not by choice. Truthfully, I had done and redone my base, blush, and liner so many times this morning that I had finally had to go with a curtailed version of the new me. Still, I had been getting compliments all day. And I loved it.

"Thank you, Max," I whispered, feeling shy all of a sudden for no apparent reason.

He grinned. "Now do you believe I'd go for you?" His hazel eyes sparkled as he waited for my answer.

"Maybe." I still wasn't convinced.

Even though people had been flattering me all day, Charlie Simpson hadn't seemed to notice the radical change in my appearance. He had barely glanced my way during English class, even though I had made sure to walk right by him on the way to my desk.

"Are you at least going to thank me for getting Shana involved?" Max asked. "She's way more help than I ever could have been."

"Shana's great," I agreed. And I was still anxious to get her help in the hair and wardrobe department.

But I loved spending time with Max. *He* was the one who had given me the confidence that allowed me to talk to Shana like she was a regular person instead of feeling totally out of her league.

Being around Max, I felt not only completely comfortable, but also one hundred percent alive. I had shared my deepest fears with a guy for the first time, and now I wasn't ready for my partnership with Max to end. Not yet.

"You know, I still know nothing about sports," I reminded Max. "Maybe you could fill me in on the basics of football and baseball. Then I'd always have something to talk about with . . . you know . . . a guy like you."

Max slapped his forehead. "Sports!" he exclaimed. "How could I have neglected such crucial territory?"

I shrugged. "I guess I have to think of everything."

"Tell you what," he suggested with a laugh. "I'll tell you everything you'll ever need to know about football and basketball over a basket of chili fries."

"Deal." On the outside, I was calm and cool, just as Max had taught me to be. But inside, I was totally excited. An afternoon with Max sounded like the perfect way to continue one of the most eventful weeks of my life.

"You did *not* eat thirteen corn dogs in one sitting," Max exclaimed. "Nobody your size could accomplish that kind of feat."

We were sitting at one of the dozens of wrought-iron tables in the middle of the mall's infamous food court. Now that Shana knew the truth, Max and I had decided that we no longer needed to go to great lengths not to be seen together. If anyone asked, we would simply say that I was "helping" Max study for a test.

I laughed. "Please—don't dare me to do it again. I felt sick for three days."

Max shook his head (I was used to the gesture by now) and gave me what I would label a "bemused" smile. "You're a constant surprise, you know that, Jane?"

I batted my eyelashes. "*Moi?* A surprise? Professor, you flatter me." I stuck another chili fry into my mouth and chewed it quickly. "Then again, I doubt Shana or Rose would do something as gauche as eating thirteen corn dogs."

"Jane, to be cool, you don't have to be like everyone else," Max informed me. "In fact, I would say just the opposite." He paused. "Anyone who can eat that much processed beef is all right with me."

I felt a warm glow. Who knew that stuffing my face with junk food on a dare from Nicole at the state fair would win me such high praise? Life was, if anything, unpredictable.

"Still, I'd rather be a cheerleader," I announced to Max. "I've never seen a pom-pom girl with no prom date."

Max rolled his eyes. "You'll have a date to the prom, Janie. Who could resist that ponytail?"

Janie. Nobody but my grandmother had ever called me Janie before. Wow. In Max's mind, I was worthy of an actual nickname. That, more than anything, made me realize how much progress I had made this week.

"Hey, the guys are here," Max declared, gazing over my shoulder. "Jane, this is a perfect opportunity for you to try flirting."

I barely heard what Max said after the words *guys* and *here* sank in. Every hair on the back of my neck stood up, and I couldn't breathe. I knew, I just *knew,* that Charlie Simpson was heading our way. This was it. Charlie was going to notice me, talk to me, think, Hey where's she been hiding for the past four years?

I used every ounce of my considerable willpower to restrain myself from turning around to confirm whether or not Charlie was one of the "guys" Max had spotted.

"Yo, Max," Brett Richmond called. "What's up?"

"Not much," Max answered. "Jane and I are chillin' with some chili fries."

Three, two, one. The guys reached our table. Brett Richmond. Jason Frango. Pitter-pat. Pitter-pat. *Charlie Simpson*.

"Hi, Jane," Brett greeted me. His voice was friendly . . . but confused. There was no doubt about it.

"Jane and I are brainstorming for one of our classes," Max explained. "And hanging out," he added, ever mindful that I not think of myself as just a study dork.

"Hi, guys." *Did those words actually come out?* I wondered. I was so nervous that my throat was totally constricted.

"Hey." Jason clearly had no idea who I was. But

I *did* notice (unless I was temporarily insane) that his eyes lingered on my face for a few more seconds than necessary. Score!

But Jason wasn't the guy who was making me feel like the laws of gravity had gone by the wayside. I looked at Charlie, willing him to talk to me.

Ideally he would pop the prom question right now, on the spot. If that didn't happen, I would have settled for a request for a date. Or a how-are-you. Or hello. *Okay, I'll settle for a nod and smile.*

"Hey," Charlie said, nodding at me.

My heart skipped several beats as all the blood in my body rushed straight to my cheeks. *You're cool. You're confident. Yet you're also flirtatious.* "Hi, Charlie."

I waited for him to say something else. *Anything.* Instead his eyes sort of glazed over and he turned to Max. "You watching the game tonight?" he asked.

"Maybe," Max answered. "I'll call you later."

Oh, to be able to casually announce one's intentions to pick up the phone and dial Charlie's number. It would be heaven! *555-6174.* I had memorized the digits almost four years ago, hoping that someday I would have a reason to use it.

"Have fun, you two," Brett said.

As the guys moved away from the table, I felt oddly deflated. Here I was, sitting with one of the most popular guys in school. And I had been acknowledged by his friends as more or less an actual person. But Charlie didn't even notice me! I might as well have been wallpaper.

The more I thought about the way Charlie's eyes had skimmed over me, the worse I felt. Even Jason hadn't really been looking at me, now that I went back over the sequence of events. He had probably been reading the big printed menu over my head.

I was, in a word, crushed. If Charlie hadn't paid any special attention to me now, he never would. The transformation was a big, fat failure.

*Max probably knows I'm hopeless,* I decided. He'd been flattering me for one reason and one reason only. He wanted to spare my feelings.

And why *wouldn't* he want to be nice to me? After all, I was the girl who was freeing up his time by writing two huge term papers for him. In theory, Max was helping transform me. In reality—he was just humoring me.

I blinked back tears. This experiment had been a joke. And I was a fool.

# Ten

## Max

SOMETHING WAS WRONG with Jane. I didn't claim to know much about girls, but I did know how to discern if a girl was trying to hold back tears. Jane's bright blue eyes glistened, and she was blinking rapidly. She was also biting her lip and avoiding my gaze.

"Jane?" I called her name softly. "What's wrong?"

She shook her head. Uh-oh. Tears were definitely imminent. I was at a total loss. Shana cried a lot (she could start gushing at the first sign that a carefully shed tear might get her what she wanted). But I knew that if Jane was about to sob, something was seriously amiss.

"Um . . . let's go take a seat on that inviting bench next to the plastic potted palm," I suggested, trying to lighten the atmosphere. "We can pretend this is Paris and we're watching the tourists stroll by."

Jane attempted a smile. "Sure. Whatever."

We left our junk-food-littered table and walked to the small, vinyl-covered bench. It wasn't exactly private, but at least it was out of the way. I took a deep breath and prepared to grill.

"Spill it," I said. "I know something is up."

"I . . . I . . . " A single tear slid down her cheek. "Never mind. It's stupid."

The sight of Jane so upset was making me queasy. I was used to her smile, her laugh. This was terrible.

"Please, Jane, tell me what's wrong. I promise I won't think it's stupid." I paused, searching for the words that would make my new friend open up to me. "And I'll do anything I can to make you feel better."

"Charlie." That was it. One word. Charlie.

*Is she speaking in code?* I wondered. I definitely needed more to go on if I was going to solve Jane's problem.

"You're not referring to Charlie Simpson for some reason, are you?" I asked hesitantly.

She nodded, her face a study in abject misery. "Yeessss." It was sort of a half wail, half sob.

"I don't understand, Janie," I said softly, hopefully maintaining a soothing, patient tone of voice. "Are you crying because we ran into Charlie? I mean, I know he's not the friendliest guy in the world. But once you get to know him, you'll like him—"

"I *do* like him," Jane interrupted. "*That's* the problem."

"You have a crush on Charlie," I stated matter-of-factly. Finally I was getting the picture. Unfortunately the queasy feeling didn't go away. If anything, it was worse.

Jane nodded. "I've had a crush on Charlie Simpson for the past four years. That's why . . ." Her voice trailed off.

"Why what?" I demanded. I sensed that I knew how Jane was going to finish the sentence. But I wanted to hear it from her lips.

"Charlie is the whole reason I wanted to do this dumb transformation," Jane admitted. "I thought that if you helped me turn into the kind of girl Charlie would be interested in . . . Well, I thought maybe he would ask me out."

Whoa. I was stunned . . . and numb. For the first time I understood Jane's determination. She wasn't embarking on this metamorphosis because of some abstract wish to fit in with the so-called cool crowd. She had a single-minded purpose.

I couldn't believe that she had gone to all of this trouble in order to *maybe* get a date with Charlie. What was so special about Charlie? Yeah, he was a good guy. And girls thought he was cute. But I had thought Jane was deeper than that. A lot deeper.

"And it's obvious that I have zero hope with him," Jane continued when I didn't say anything. "He barely even glanced in my direction when he stopped by our table! If he didn't notice me then, he's *never* going to."

"Jane . . ." But I didn't know what to say. She was so distraught.

"Thanks for all of your help, Max. Really. But this whole thing was a total mistake."

I wanted to reassure Jane. But I was still stuck on the fact that she had been pining for Charlie since, apparently, the dawn of time. I just couldn't believe it. *What am I feeling?* It was a combination of nausea, shock, and something that felt a lot like anger. Or at least irritation.

*Could I be jealous?* The thought popped into my head before I could stop it. But no. That was impossible. I had a girlfriend. I was madly in love with Shana. So it didn't make any sense that I could be jealous of Jane's feelings for Charlie.

I was surprised. That was all. And okay, I was feeling a little protective about Jane. I didn't like to see her hurting this way. And indirectly at least, Charlie was responsible for the tears that had rolled down her cheeks.

"This hasn't been for nothing," I insisted. "You know it hasn't. And I'm sure that Charlie *will* notice you. Give him a little time."

Suddenly Jane sat up ramrod straight. "Max, you have to *swear* that you won't tell anyone that I have a crush on Charlie. *Nobody.* Not even Shana."

Obviously getting a date with Charlie meant more to Jane than almost anything else in the world. I was her friend, and it was my duty to do whatever I could to make her dream come true.

It was the least I could do for a person who had,

somehow, done a lot to open up my world in ways I never would have guessed even a week ago. She'd given me opera and bowling. *And I'll deliver Charlie Simpson.*

"I won't tell a soul," I promised. "But I do have a great idea about how to get Charlie to notice you."

"I don't know. . . ." Jane stared off into the distance, contemplating my words.

"Do you trust me?" I asked. "If you do, you'll let me help you."

She gave me the kind of half smile I had come to recognize meant Jane was nervous but hopeful. "Okay," she announced.

And with that simple statement, I had a mission.

I was still thinking about my conversation with Jane when the doorbell rang at my house at ten o'clock that night. But all thoughts of Jane flew out of my head when I saw Shana's angry face. Something was up—and all signs suggested that whatever it was had to do with me.

"Hi, sweetie," I greeted her. "It's so awesome to see you." I held out my arms and silently prayed that Shana would walk right into them.

She didn't. "Mind if I come in?" she asked, her voice icy cold. "Or do you have company?"

I opened the door even wider. "Of course. I mean, no, I don't have anyone here." Being confronted by a girl's anger always turns me into a blithering idiot. "Come inside."

Shana breezed past me and stalked toward the

living room. "Cut the act, Max," she commanded. "Madison saw you."

"Saw me?" I asked. "Saw me . . . *what?*"

Shana perched at the edge of the sofa, but she looked like a tightly wound coil, ready to spring at any moment. "You were spotted at the mall with another girl this afternoon." If her tone was ominous, her eyes were outright stormy.

I laughed. "That was Jane," I assured her. "We went to the mall to talk sports. You know, working on the project."

Shana raised one eyebrow. "According to Madison, you two looked *very* friendly."

This day had been crazy. First I found out that Jane's whole reason for *being* was to go on a date with Charlie Simpson. Now Shana was going postal due to an innocent sighting of Jane and me at the mall. This was insane.

There was nothing going on between Jane and me. Nothing. And it was annoying that Shana would even *suggest* otherwise.

"Of course we looked friendly," I told her. "We've become *friends.*"

My tone had sounded a lot more hostile than I intended. I was practically shouting. *De Nile ain't just a river in Egypt, Max,* I said to myself. But despite the emotions that were whirling inside me, I had to stay focused on the facts. I had a girlfriend. And Jane had a major crush on one of my best friends.

I shook my head, clearing out the confusing, conflicting messages that my heart was sending to my brain. Clearly I had spent too much time in the company of girls this week. I was getting *way* analytical.

"Max, I think you're wasting entirely too much time on your little charity case," Shana snapped. "It's . . . well, it's pathetic."

A sharp pang of irritation caused most of the muscles in my body to tense up. "Shana, Jane is *not* pathetic. And neither am I."

"Whatever." She gave me a tight smile that was anything but sincere. "From now on, I'll take over your loser friend's attempt at being a real person."

I had been prepared to grovel. I had been prepared to soothe Shana's hurt feelings. But there was no chance that I was going to sit here and listen to her bad-mouth Jane. Maybe Shana didn't see Jane for who she really was, but *I* did. And I was going to make sure that Charlie did too.

"Jane is *not* a charity case," I stated (hopefully for the last time). "She's a really cool person, and she's a friend." I paused. "In fact, I was thinking . . . well, that we should set up Jane on a date."

Shana flopped onto the couch and sighed dramatically. "With whom, might I ask?"

"With Charlie," I suggested. "He's single, she's single. . . . It's a perfect match." Silently I willed Shana to agree with me.

She snorted. "Face facts, Max. There is no way that Charlie would be interested in Jane—even if she does look better, thanks to my help."

I stared at my girlfriend's beautiful face. Usually the moment I looked into her eyes, I caved. She wanted to see a chick flick? Fine with me. She wanted me to order a vegetarian soy burger instead of the baby-back ribs? Fine with me. She needed a ride to school at six-thirty in the morning for an emergency cheerleading practice? Fine with me.

But at this moment I knew that no amount of hugs, kisses, or cajoling was going to deter me from my goal. "Charlie *will* like Jane," I insisted. "And I'll prove it to you—we'll all go on a double date, and you can see for yourself."

"This should be interesting," Shana responded, flipping her hair. "Sort of like watching a train wreck."

I sat down beside Shana and put my arm around her. "We'll have a blast," I assured her. "We can all go bowling and eat nachos and play Foosball."

Shana turned her head. She gave me a you-are-crazier-than-I-ever-dreamed-possible look. *"Bowling?"*

Oops. *I forgot that bowling isn't cool.* But *why* wasn't bowling cool? It was fun, harmless, and a lot cheaper than dinner at La Fondue or some other stuffy, overheated restaurant.

Actually, a lot of things that were considered un-cool were really fun. Chess, for instance. I had been a member of the chess club freshman year, and I had loved it. And then varsity football and baseball had come along . . . and everybody told me that it was dorky for a jock to be in the chess club. I had dutifully quit . . . but why? *Not because I don't like to play chess anymore,* I realized.

Huh. For the first time in a long time I was thinking about what I *really* enjoyed and what I had been *told* to enjoy. Was it possible that I had lost a sense of myself to the degree that I didn't even know my own tastes?

*I'm going to change that,* I decided. From now on I was going to listen to my own heart—not to other people's heads!

# Eleven

## Jane

"JANE, I'VE BEEN wanting to do this for a long time." He put his hands on my waist, drawing me closer and closer to his broad chest.

It was late at night, and we were all alone in the Union High library. The only light came from a small lamp on one of the study tables. Aside from our voices and the sound of our breathing, the room was bathed in silence.

"I don't know . . . ," I whispered softly. But I was powerless to resist as his full, red lips neared mine.

I wanted this kiss. I wanted it more than anything in the whole world. I closed my eyes as his lips touched mine. Electric sparks traveled up and down my spine, leaving me breathless. After what was either forever or only a brief second, he pulled away.

"Jane, put your hair up in that cute ponytail and

*scrub off all the makeup that's hiding your beautiful face,"* he whispered. *"And then tell me you'll go to the prom with me. . . . Please, say yes."*

*"Yes, Max . . . yes . . ."*

My eyes popped open, and I found myself staring into the dark. I had been dreaming about . . . Max. *Max!* I sat straight up in bed, my heart pounding. The sheets were twisted around my body, and the comforter had fallen to the floor. But I was clutching my pillow tightly to my chest.

Remembering the image of Max's face from my dream sent flutters dancing up and down my nerve endings. It was exactly the same sensation that I felt every time I encountered Charlie in the hallway at school. Or in English class. Or in the cafeteria.

But I hadn't been dreaming about Charlie. It had been Max who was kissing me. And Max who I had dreamed of asking me to the prom. *Why is this happening?*

Max wasn't the guy I longed for. Charlie was. Just today at the mall I had felt that uncontrollable flutter when Charlie approached our table.

Hadn't I? Second by second, I replayed in my mind the entire encounter. Max had said that the guys were there. My heart had stopped (basically). My palms had started to sweat. But . . . but . . . what I felt was . . . anxiety. And nerves. And fear. *Not* The Flutter.

My eyes were beginning to adjust to the darkness, but as I looked around my room, it was as if I were seeing everything for the first time. And it wasn't just the dresser and the nightstand and my old teddy bear that looked new to me. It was *me*. And my entire life.

I thought about how upset I had been when Charlie hadn't noticed me the way I had hoped he would. Had the tears I shed been for *Charlie?* Or had the tears been for the failure of my transformation? That's what Charlie's lack of flirting represented to me, I realized. That even transformed, I still wasn't the kind of girl a guy like Max would go for.

Somewhere along the way I had stopped caring quite so much whether or not Charlie asked me to the prom. Sure, I still told myself that I cared. But it wasn't the same all-consuming desire that had forced me to approach Max that day in the library.

Instead I had become consumed with the idea of transforming myself. Of becoming the *kind* of girl who guys like Max and Charlie would go for. I had wanted to accomplish something concrete with my metamorphosis. I had wanted to gain something I could hold on to, now and in the future.

The fact that Charlie's eyes hadn't rested on me for more than the requisite half second had con-firmed my worst fears—that Plain Jane Smith could never be anything more. Even trying my hardest, I had been unable to attract the kind of guy who would make me feel special, who would make me stand out.

At least before, when I had been my boring, inconspicuous self, I could dream of the day when things would be different. I had been a bundle of potential, believing that I always had a chance at being an "it" girl.

Now I had tried. And I had failed. No matter what, I would never be the kind of girl who Max or Charlie would ask to the prom . . . or anywhere else that mattered. It wasn't just about this week or next week.

I had a long life of *not* standing out to look forward to. In college . . . after college . . . my life would be a series of boring nonadventures, designed to highlight me as the reliable, straight-A student who nobody felt inspired to invite to a party.

I slumped back into my pillows and pulled the covers up over my head. Hot tears forced their way out of my eyes. All I wanted to do was hide from the world forever, safe inside my cocoon, where I could cry in peace.

As far as I could tell, I had nothing—and no one—to look forward to.

"I never thought I'd like working at Cherie's," Nicole commented. "But the pay isn't bad, and the dresses are gorgeous. It's too bad I'm not going to the prom—I get a twenty percent employee discount."

Nicole had recently started to work at the most expensive dress shop in the mall. She was determined to save enough money in the next four months to buy herself a used car to take to college.

"You should see these girls, shopping for prom dresses." Nicole said, shaking her head. "You'd think that since the day they were born, the only thing they've been waiting to do is shop for a strapless taffeta sheath." She paused. "Speaking of taffeta, you should come take a look around the shop, Jane. You've got to be ready when Charlie pops the big question."

"I'll pass," I told Nicole, unwrapping the cellophane from what was passing for my lunch.

"How can you eat that stuff?" Christy asked, wrinkling her nose as she surveyed my nutrition-free selection.

I had bypassed the limp green salad, chicken à la king, and strawberry Jell-O that the cafeteria was offering for lunch on Friday. Instead I was digging into a pack of overly processed cupcakes I had bought from the vending machine. My mood called for junk food. Period.

"For the next two days I will eat only potato chips and chocolate products," I informed Christy. "I'm declaring a moratorium on healthy living."

Nicole frowned at the piece of gray chicken that she was about to put into her mouth. "This can't be a part of Operation Glam Girl. I figured from now on you'd be eating tofu burgers and soy shakes."

I stuffed another bite of cupcake into my mouth, shaking my head. "Nope. I'm abandoning the trans-formation end of my deal with Max. It's hopeless."

"But Jane, you were so excited. I mean, just yesterday you said you had found your 'inner homecoming queen,'" Christy pointed out.

I felt like cringing. How could I have said something so stupid?

"I'm Plain Jane Smith, and I always will be," I announced to my friends. "The Maxes of this world are not there for my taking."

Nicole raised her eyebrows. "*Maxes?*" she asked. "I thought you wanted *Charlie.*"

"Uh . . . did I say Max?" I felt my face turn bright red. Jeez. I had been embarrassed so many times this week that my face was a perma-tomato. "I meant Charlie. Definitely Charlie."

I didn't bother to add that I'd had a more-than-friendly dream about none other than Max Ziff just last night. I had bared my soul enough for one week. Enough for a lifetime. From now on, I was going to keep my pathetic fantasy life to myself.

"Charlie is an idiot if doesn't notice you," Christy stated firmly. "He should consider himself the luckiest guy at Union High that you've got a crush on him."

I shrugged, sick to death of the entire subject. "Can we drop it?" I asked. "I just want to be me for a while."

Nicole pushed aside her plate of chicken and grabbed one of my cupcakes. "Well, I, for one, am not sorry to see you letting go of this whole makeover extravaganza."

"Yeah, Jane," Christy added. "We like you just the way you are—were—thank you very much."

I smiled at my friends, despite the sadness inside me. Nicole and Christy loved me unconditionally—and for now, that would have to do. Actually, I didn't really mind giving up my dreams of buying an all-new wardrobe and spending half an hour a day doing my hair and makeup.

But . . . but something was bumming me out in a major way. *It's Max,* I realized. I had gotten used to hanging out with him. And I was going to miss it. I was going to miss it more than I ever would have imagined.

"Janie, I've been looking all over for you!" Max's exuberant voice broke into my thoughts as I walked toward my sixth-period precalculus class.

"Hey, Max." I had been more or less avoiding him all day. After my bizarre dream I needed to get my head together.

He was grinning and apparently oblivious to my less-than-enthusiastic greeting. "Tell me you're free tomorrow night." He paused. "No, that's not right. I'm telling *you* that you've got to be free tomorrow night. If you have plans, you *must* cancel them."

"Uh . . . why?" I had never seen him so excited. "What's going on?"

Max looked ready to burst. "You have a date. Actually, it's a double date, with me and Shana . . . and Charlie Simpson!"

My jaw dropped. I tried to ignore the ringing in my ears and focus on what Max had just said. This couldn't be happening! But the look on Max's face assured me that I wasn't hallucinating. He had managed the impossible.

So much for abandoning my project. There was no way I could turn Max down. Not when he looked this excited and had done me a huge "favor."

"Oh!" What else was there to say?

"And tomorrow, Shana wants to take you shopping for some date-worthy clothes." He reached out and squeezed my shoulder. "So is this great, or is this great?"

I nodded. "It's great," I echoed. But more than anything, I felt shocked and afraid. Uncomfortable.

"Listen, if Charlie doesn't fall for you on Saturday night, then there's something seriously wrong with him," Max said softly.

As I watched him walk away, I leaned against a bank of lockers and pressed my cheek against the cool metal. What was wrong with me? Just yesterday I had been completely depressed because I was convinced that the transformation hadn't been effective.

Now I had received the supposed best news of my life, but all I could think about was Max. And he was the person who had told me again and again that he liked the way I looked *before* I started my metamorphosis. At least, that's what he'd claimed.

*But this is good,* I told myself. I had gotten what I wanted. A date with Charlie Simpson. This was the culmination of everything Max and I had been working for.

So I was going to get psyched about my date— and force myself to quit thinking about Max. He was off-limits. Max had a girlfriend—one who had been incredibly helpful to me. Guilt washed over me as I remembered the dream I'd had the night before.

"Charlie is the one I want," I whispered aloud. "Charlie."

# Twelve

## Jane

"GIVE HER SOME highlights, Jamie," Shana instructed my hairdresser on Saturday afternoon. "We've got to do something about that dishwater-blond hair."

Jamie—whose hair was a beautiful, curly, red mane that any girl would have envied—studied my face. "Yes, we need to lighten you up," she declared. "We'll bring out the eyes and the cheekbones with some layers around your face."

I opened my mouth to respond. Did I *want* highlights and layers? "I don't know—"

"You'll love it," Jamie assured me. "An hour and a half from now you'll walk out of here looking like a supermodel."

Before I could say another word, she tipped back my chair. A moment later I felt warm water running over my head, drowning out the sound of everything else going on around me.

For the first time all day I began to feel relaxed. Ever since I'd met Shana in front of the mall two hours ago, I'd been plunged into a whirlwind of activity. Shana had taken me from store to store, giving me piles of clothes to try on in each one.

With a simple thumbs-up or thumbs-down, she would declare whether or not my outfit was worthy of purchase. Seven shops, one Wonderbra, and five credit card purchases later, I was ready not only for my date tonight but for dates well into my twenties.

Adrenaline had pumped through my veins as we left the last shop and headed toward the salon. Spending a lot of money on amazing clothes had made me feel, for the first time, like a normal, healthy teenager. And I had loved every second of it.

*If Shana thinks I need highlights, I need highlights,* I decided as Jamie massaged shampoo into my thin hair. I trusted Shana's instincts implicitly.

Jamie turned off the water and tilted my chair upright. As she toweled my hair dry, I smiled at Shana in the huge mirror that lined one wall of the salon.

"Good-bye, dishwater blond," I said to Shana.

She grinned. "Jamie does wonders," she informed me. "*Everyone* comes here to get their hair done."

"Thanks again for doing all of this for me, Shana," I said as Jamie pulled a comb through my hair. "I never could have prepared for this date without you."

"No problem." Shana smiled at me from her chair. "Speaking of the date, Max never got a

110

chance to fill me in on the details. I mean, how did this thing even come together?"

"I'm not sure," I answered honestly. Thursday afternoon Max had promised that he would get Charlie to notice me, and less than twenty-four hours later he had arranged the date. I hadn't bothered to ask who, what, when, why, where, or how.

"Well, whose idea was it?" Shana asked. "Did you suggest it? Or did Max?"

"Um . . ." I didn't know how to respond.

The idea of admitting my long-standing crush on Charlie Simpson wasn't exactly appealing. Enough people—well, me and three others—knew that I had harbored a thing for him. I didn't want to advertise my abiding desire to sit across from him during a dinner date.

"Come on, Jane," Shana pressed. "You can tell me. We're friends."

*How can I argue with that?* I wondered. Shana had gone out of her way to help me with Girl 101. I owed her my trust. And my friendship. So what if she hadn't been nice in the past? Now that Shana had gotten to know me, she realized that I was a cool person after all.

I smiled sheepishly, and once again I was positive that the dreaded blush had crept into my cheeks. "Well . . . I guess the date with Charlie was *my* idea—indirectly."

"What do you mean?" Shana asked. "I want to hear the whole story—and don't leave out any of the gory details."

111

As Jamie tipped my head and slathered my hair with something that looked like wet concrete, I searched for the right words with which to explain my feelings for Charlie.

"Well . . . the other day I confessed to Max that I've had a crush on Charlie since the summer after eighth grade," I said, going straight to the point. "I didn't want to tell him, but Max sort of pried the secret out of me."

"Hmmm . . . interesting." Shana nodded. "So what did Max say when you told him?"

I smiled, remembering the moment. "He was totally understanding. He said Charlie would be crazy not to want to date me, and then he said he had an idea about how to get us together." I paused. "But I never thought it would actually happen."

"Wow. You and Max have gotten close," Shana commented. "It sounds like you two tell each other everything."

I nodded. "You must feel like the luckiest girl in the world to have Max as your boyfriend," I commented. "He's probably the nicest guy I've ever met."

"I am lucky," Shana agreed. "And so are you." She flipped the magazine she was reading shut and stared right at me. "I mean, it wasn't easy for Max to convince Charlie to go on this date," Shana said. "But Max believes in his 'cause' so much that he managed to do it."

"Uh . . . oh." My heart was sinking straight to my feet. Had Max really had to twist Charlie's arm to make him go out with me? That was more humiliating than if I had never gotten the chance to go out with him at all!

Either way Shana had insulted me. Hadn't she?

"You know, this haircut is going to look so amazing!" Shana trilled, as if she hadn't one second ago said something that she knew would hurt my feelings. "I can't wait to see how it looks after Jamie does the blow-dry!"

Huh. Shana sounded so friendly, so sincerely excited about tonight. Maybe I had heard her wrong before. Yes. That must have been it. Shana wasn't the *most* sensitive person in the world. But I knew she would never say anything to deliberately hurt me. If she didn't like me, she wouldn't have involved herself in my transformation in the first place.

I pushed the uneasy feeling away and concentrated on tonight. With my new clothes, my new makeup, my new hair, and my new form-enhancing Wonderbra, Charlie Simpson was finally going to see Plain Jane Smith in a whole new light.

I just hoped I didn't trip over my chair or spill soup in my lap!

"Which earrings should I wear? The silver hoops or the rhinestone studs?" I held up one of each pair of earrings for Nicole and Christy to inspect.

"The hoops," Nicole declared. "They're sexy yet casual."

I had called my friends an hour and a half ago and begged them to come over for an emergency pep-talk session. So far, they had managed to keep me calm enough that I hadn't thrown up.

"Does my mascara look okay?" I asked. "I don't want to get that raccoon thing happening."

Christy laughed. "Jane, you look beautiful! Just relax."

"It's kind of hard to relax in this dress," I admitted to my friends. "It's so tight that I feel like I'm wearing a dress-sized rubber band."

"You could always change into jeans and a T-shirt," Nicole suggested.

"Ha!" I responded. "I'd rather spend the next few hours holding my breath than discard my new image."

Because the outfit looked good. Actually, it looked great. Pink, tight, and sleeveless, the dress fell to just below my knees. I had added a pair of high, silver, strappy sandals that made me at least three inches taller. So what if it felt like I was walking on stilts? My legs looked awesome!

Nicole glanced at her watch. "Uh-oh. Christy and I had better get out of here. Unless you want your two ugly stepsisters hanging around when Prince Charming shows up."

"Thanks for helping me out," I told my friends. "I don't think I could have gotten through the last two hours of powdering, puffing, and primping without you two."

"I hope Charlie knows how lucky he is," Christy said, giving me a warm hug. "You deserve the best."

"Be sure not to chew with your mouth open, and you'll be fine," Nicole advised me, grinning.

"Got it." I hugged her close, wishing I could take

Nicole and Christy along on the date for moral support.

A moment later my friends were gone, and I was left alone with my sweaty palms and nervous stomach. The clock was ticking. There was no way I could back out of the date now even if I wanted to.

I stood in front of the full-length mirror in my room. My makeup was perfect. My hair looked great (I loved the way Jamie had framed my face with subtle layers). The jewelry was right. And the dress . . . Well, I practically felt naked. Which was probably a good sign.

*I don't look exactly like Shana and her friends,* I thought, studying myself from every angle. There was some inherent, intangible element missing from my appearance. But I definitely looked cool and sophisticated—a whole new me.

*I wonder if Max will like this dress,* I thought, tugging on the hem. And then I froze. Max. Max. Max. Everything always came back to him.

"Stop it, Jane," I ordered myself. "Stop thinking about you-know-who."

I picked up my brand-new blush brush to do a final touch-up. But the doorbell rang before I could apply any more makeup.

"I can do this, I can do this, I can do this." I repeated the phrase like a mantra as I grabbed my purse and raced down the stairs.

I stopped in front of the door, pasted on a smile, and took a long, deep breath. *Good luck, Jane,* I told myself. And then I opened the door.

Standing in front of me were Max, Shana . . . and

Charlie. Until this second I hadn't been one hundred percent convinced that Charlie would actually show. But he had. Clad in pressed khakis and a light blue shirt that brought out the color of his eyes, Charlie looked as gorgeous as I had ever seen him.

My heart pounded as I realized that this was *it*. Tonight I would find out once and for all if I had what it took to attract a guy like Charlie Simpson.

I froze again, for just a second, as I realized that Charlie had gone from dream guy to the embodiment of everything I didn't think I could ever really have, transformed or not.

After tonight I would know one way or the other. Either way—bad or good—I would have my answer.

Everything would be okay . . . as long as I remembered to breathe!

# Thirteen

## Max

"WE'RE HERE," I announced, pulling into the parking lot of C & O Trattoria, one of the nicest Italian restaurants in town.

I glanced into the rearview mirror for the tenth time, trying to gauge how things were going between Jane and Charlie. He was sitting *really* close to her. They barely knew each other, but Charlie wasn't wasting any time. He was cracking one (unfunny) joke after another, trying to impress Jane with his charm.

But that was good. Right? Right. I wanted Jane to be happy, to get what she wanted. But . . . but . . . what? *Why am I having a problem with this?* I asked myself.

"I assume you made reservations," Shana proclaimed, climbing out of the car. "This place is always packed on Saturday night."

"Uh . . ." Oops. I had neglected that small detail.

"Don't worry about it, Max," Jane told me, slamming the car door shut. "We can hang out and talk while we wait for a table."

"This guy. You can't take him anywhere." Charlie pounded me on the back. Then he slung an arm around me and bent his head close to mine. "Dude, she's pretty hot," he whispered loudly.

"Yeah. I know." For some reason I wasn't in a Saturday-night kind of mood as we walked en masse into the fancy restaurant.

"Ziff. Party of four," Shana informed the tuxe-doed maitre d'. "And we would like a table by the window. I don't want to be stuck next to the kitchen like I was the last time I was here."

The maitre d' bowed. "Of course, miss." But I noticed a pained expression on his face as he wrote my name down on a small white tablet.

"We'd better not have to wait more than fifteen minutes," Shana declared. "Otherwise I'm going straight to the manager."

I didn't bother to respond. I had learned from past experience that once Shana had started to complain about restaurant conditions, the safest thing to do was to let her ramble until she got what she wanted.

While Shana was frowning and wrinkling her nose, Jane was positively beaming. She looked around the restaurant as if she were seeing the Sistine Chapel for the first time.

"I love these stained-glass windows," she said to

Charlie. "I feel like I'm actually in Italy." She became totally still for a moment, then cupped a hand around her ear. "Max, they're playing *La Bohème*!"

"La *what?*" Charlie asked, looking bewildered.

"Oh . . . never mind," Jane responded quickly. "It's just this dumb opera that Max and I were laughing about the other day."

I knew Jane was lying. She *loved* opera. But how could I fault her? She was only acting the way *I* had taught her to.

"Max, will you get me a diet Coke from the bar?" Shana more commanded than asked. "The air is so dry in here that I'm absolutely *parched.*"

I dutifully headed toward the restaurant's small bar. But I was feeling crankier than ever. Sometimes I wished Shana could be a little more . . . well, a little more like Jane. Down-to-earth. And it would be pleasant if she were more appreciative of the world around her. Unlike Jane, Shana tended to search for the negative in any situation and then point it out for everybody else to notice.

"Tell them not to put too much ice in my soda!" Shana called after me.

I cringed. *It wouldn't hurt if my girlfriend were a little* nicer *too,* I reflected. As I approached the bar, I realized how weird the whirl of thoughts in my brain was.

The whole point of the deal Jane and I had made was to turn Jane into a girl like *Shana* so that a guy like me would go for her. *But a guy like me would go for Jane just as she is!*

And then it hit me. What Jane had needed wasn't a so-called transformation. Not at all. What Jane *did* need was access. Up until now she had never had the chance to spend any significant amount of time with guys like Charlie and me. But once a guy got to know her and realized how great she was, of course he would be interested!

Well, tonight Jane was getting exactly the opportunity she had needed all along. She would be sitting at a table with Charlie, and she would have his full attention. This was it! Jane was about to fulfill her dream. . . . *So why do I feel so lousy?*

By the time we sat down twenty minutes later, I had progressed from merely hungry to totally starving. *That's probably why I'm in such a bad mood,* I thought. Hunger.

I was seated next to Shana and across from Jane. Good. This way if Jane got nervous, I could cast her encouraging glances across the table. I was going to be supportive, no matter *how* cranky these hunger pangs were making me.

"Hi, my name is Olga," our waitress greeted us. "I'll be your server tonight."

"Olga?" Charlie asked. "That doesn't sound Italian. . . . Are you sure you're qualified to work here?"

Olga raised an eyebrow. "You don't look old enough to be able to afford an expensive meal. . . . Are you sure you're qualified to *eat* here?" She stuck out her hip and batted her eyelashes.

I resisted the urge to roll my eyes. Yeah, I believed in being friendly to waitresses. But I didn't approve of Charlie's overly familiar style of banter. It was . . . sort of embarrassing.

I glanced at Jane, but she seemed totally oblivious. She was carefully studying the menu, expressing delight over several of the dishes.

Luckily Olga started to recite tonight's specials, so Charlie didn't have the chance to pelt her with another insult slash come-on.

"And finally, we have a special pesto pizza that comes with eggplant and sun-dried tomatoes," Olga concluded a full two minutes later.

Charlie leaned forward in his chair. "What, no oysters?" he asked. "We were all hoping for an aphrodisiac to get us in the *mood*."

Olga giggled. "Seems to me like you're *already* in the mood."

Now I really was embarrassed. I hated it when Charlie pulled out this immature mating ritual—especially on a date! He should have been giving all of his attention to Jane, not the well-endowed waitress.

But nobody else seemed bothered. Shana was giggling behind her napkin, and Jane still seemed to be absorbed in her menu. *Take it easy, Max,* I told myself. *Just have a good time—like you're supposed to.*

After we did our round of ordering, I grabbed a piece of hot, fresh garlic bread from the basket in the middle of the table. I was positive that as soon as I had something in my stomach, I would be able to lighten up.

Once Olga was gone, Charlie shifted his focus squarely onto Jane. He turned around in his chair so that they were looking at each other straight in the eyes. Now—this was more like it!

"How come you haven't been around more, Jane?" Charlie asked. "I can't believe I've never noticed you before."

"Oh, uh, we actually have a class together," Jane told Charlie. "English with Mr. Atkison."

He snapped his fingers. "*Right.* Jane Smith, literary genius." He squinted in her direction. "Is it true that you're the smartest girl in the whole school?"

Jane's face turned a soft, pretty red. "I don't know. I mean, no, of course not—"

"Do brains like to have fun?" Charlie interrupted. "Like, how far have you gone with a guy?"

"Uh . . . what?" Jane's face was now bordering on crimson, and I felt like punching Charlie in the middle of his ruggedly handsome face.

He snorted with laughter. "Just kidding!" He pounded the table. "But I had you going, huh?"

I felt like slipping out of my seat and spending the rest of the evening hiding under the table. Shana could feed me rolls, and I could have Olga set down my chicken marsala on the floor.

But I couldn't abandon Jane now. She was glancing at each of us in turn, and I got the feeling that she was racking her brain for something now. So far, she hadn't contributed much to the conversation—except for Charlie, nobody had had the chance to get a word in edgewise.

Jane cleared her throat, and we all looked at her expectantly. "So, um, Charlie, have you read that book by Jon Krakauer, *Into Thin Air*?"

"Nope. Never heard of it." Charlie took a bite of garlic bread and chewed contentedly.

"Oh," Jane said, sounding disappointed. "I thought you might have because it's sort of a 'guys' book. It's about a group of people who climbed Mount Everest—"

"Sounds boring," Shana interrupted. "I'd rather read about romance and intrigue than a bunch of nature buffs."

"I read the book," I told Jane. "It was awesome. I felt like I was on the mountain with all of those people while they fought for their lives."

Jane's eyes lit up. "Have you seen the IMAX movie of Everest?" she asked me.

"Yes!" I exclaimed. "I went back twice." Of course, I tried to get Shana to go to the movie with me, but she refused to see any film that didn't star either Julia Roberts or Cameron Diaz.

"The giant IMAX screen is so amazing," Jane continued. "I loved the one about the deep sea. . . . It was the closest I've ever been to scuba diving."

I wished I could talk to Shana about this kind of stuff. I loved exchanging views about movies and books, but somehow those subjects never came up when Shana and I were on a date.

*What* do *we talk about?* I wondered, turning to look at my beautiful, popular girlfriend.

Shana caught my gaze. She gave me a megawatt

smile and leaned forward. A moment later she snaked her arms around my waist and gave me a kiss on the lips.

"Now, that's better than any stupid movie," Shana declared.

I nodded. But . . . did I really agree?


"So . . . what do you think of Jane?" I asked Charlie when the girls took off for what Shana called the "powder room" in between dinner and dessert.

Charlie pursed his lips, scanning the dessert menu. "Huh." He mulled over the question. "She's cute. I think I'm going to have the tiramisu."

"I *know* she's cute," I answered, feeling a wave of frustration. "But do you *like* her? You know, really *like* her."

Charlie shrugged. "She's kind of boring—not really my type."

"Boring?" I echoed. In my experience Jane was a lot of things—boring wasn't one of them.

"Yeah . . . like, she didn't laugh at any of my jokes." Charlie was warming up to his subject now. "And I was doing some really good stuff!"

In my opinion, Charlie's jokes hadn't been all that funny. In fact, if I had to apply the word *boring* to any of us, it would have been him. Or maybe *boorish* was the better word. But I wasn't about to share my thoughts with Charlie—after all, he was one of my best friends. Most of the time.

"That's too bad," I replied instead. "But you know, maybe it'll just take a little more time for you

124

two to get comfortable with each other. Jane really is an awesome chick."

"Maybe." Charlie didn't seem too concerned with the outcome of his date. He was probably wondering what the baseball score was.

I wasn't sure how to feel about Charlie's lukewarm reaction to Jane. Part of me was relieved. Deep down, I didn't believe that Charlie was good enough for Jane—friend of mine or not.

But another part of me was disappointed. This date meant so much to Jane. I was sorry that Charlie hadn't immediately fallen head over heels in love with her, as I was sure she wanted him to.

I sighed deeply, suddenly not feeling so hungry for dessert. This "bargain" with Jane had turned into something a lot more complicated than I ever could have imagined.

# Fourteen

## Jane

FRESHLY LIP GLOSSED and powdered, I followed Shana toward our table. *I should have said more to Shana while we were redoing our makeup,* I realized, my gaze on the straight line of the other girl's back. Girl talk was an essential element of a double date, right?

But I had been too busy making sure I didn't smudge my mascara to do much chitchatting. Besides, what would I have said? My emotions and thoughts were so scattered that even *I* wasn't sure what I was thinking.

We got to the table . . . and my eyes immediately went to Max. I almost gasped when I saw that he was staring right back at me. I had never seen him look so *intense*. I could barely breathe as we looked into each other's eyes. Three. Two. One. I forced my gaze to move from Max to Charlie—where it should have been all along.

What was wrong with me anyway? Tonight was my big chance with Charlie—the culmination of everything I had been dreaming about for four years. But so far I had spent most of the night making mental notes about how good Max's dark green shirt looked on him. The color made his hazel eyes appear a deep, aqua green.

And I couldn't stop thinking about how much Max and I had in common, how much we had to talk about. Books, movies, music . . . I felt like I could talk to Max forever and never run out of things to say.

Yes, the only reason I was even at this restaurant, on this date, was because I had been in love with Charlie since forever. But . . . but . . . every time Shana leaned over to kiss Max, I felt as if someone were driving a knife through my heart.

*I am seriously deranged,* I decided. *This is categorically nuts!* I simply had to ignore these confusing feelings and focus on my goal. From this moment forward, I was going to put into practice every single thing Max had taught me. I would use my newfound womanly wiles to drive Charlie mad with desire!

"Hi, guys, did you miss us?" I asked, batting my eyelashes in Charlie's direction.

"Uh . . . yeah." He sat up a little straighter and reached over to pull out my chair.

I slipped into my chair, crossed my legs at the ankles (in true ladylike fashion), and fixed my attention on Charlie.

"Have you two decided on dessert?" Shana asked, placing her hand in Max's and leaning her body against his.

"Personally, I'm stuffed," I informed the table. "Charlie, is it okay if I just have a bite of whatever you order?"

"Yeah. Yes, of course." He flashed me the same smile that had made me fall for him all those years ago.

"So, Charlie, have you seen any good bands lately?" I asked.

"Yeah! I went to see Radio Active at Wally's the other night. They totally rocked!"

"I've been dying to see them!" I declared, my voice practically bursting with enthusiasm. "I wish I'd known Radio Active was playing—I definitely would have checked them out."

Lies. Lies. Lies. I had never heard of the band or, for that matter, of Wally's. But I doubted that Charlie was going to grill me on the subject. And for the first time tonight he actually seemed interested in something I had to say. This was getting kind of fun.

"The Ringmasters are playing next week," Charlie told me. "But I can't go—we've got a big game against JFK High."

"Bummer!" *Note to self: Research the Ringmasters on the Internet.*

"Tell me about it," Charlie answered, sounding crestfallen. "But hey, them's the breaks. If we want to have a shot at the major leagues, we've got to be dedicated."

Huh? Did Charlie really think he was going to

128

be a professional baseball player? I couldn't imagine wanting to spend that much time around guys whose main hobby was spitting on AstroTurf.

The conversation continued. Charlie threw out the names of bands, cafés, and Web sites, and I responded accordingly. Luckily I had gotten enough coaching from Max that I actually had something to say about the majority of the bands Charlie mentioned.

But my heart wasn't really in it. Sure, I enjoyed the fact that Charlie Simpson appeared to be flirting with me. And mindless banter wasn't all bad—I laughed several times. Yet . . . I knew this kind of interaction would never be enough for me. Not for hours on end.

I liked *real* conversation. I liked to debate, and argue, and have my ideas challenged to the point that I had to question my own beliefs. Somehow I didn't think Charlie would be thrilled at the prospect of an in-depth discussion of a presidential election.

"You should go to Langly's Coffee Shop sometime," Charlie was saying. "They serve free chocolate-chip cookies every Tuesday night. . . ."

As I nodded along to Charlie's steady stream of conversation, I allowed myself to steal a quick glance at Max, who was talking quietly with Shana on the other side of the table.

I expected him to shoot me an encouraging smile or a discreet victory sign. But he didn't. In fact, he didn't even look in my direction. He was staring at some point over Shana's shoulder . . . and he looked, well . . . glum.

I moved my gaze from Max to Shana. She was frowning at her water glass, and I noticed that she was biting her lip. Weird.

I looked back at Charlie, who was still mid-story. But my mind wasn't on his words. Instead I was worrying about the progress of the night. Charlie seemed oblivious to everything but his own jokes, but Max and Shana clearly weren't enjoying themselves.

Was it my fault? Had I done something wrong? And if so . . . what?

I didn't say much during the short drive from the C & O Trattoria to my house. I sat in the dark backseat with Charlie, half listening to the detailed discussion he and Max were having about the various baseball recruiters who had been showing up at practice. Shana hadn't said more than three words since we'd left the restaurant.

"Here we are, Jane," Max announced, pulling up in front of my house. "We have delivered you safely to your abode."

"Thanks, everybody," I said. "I had a great time."

As I opened the door of the car, I half expected Max to get out and walk me to the door. After all, he was the person in the car who I had the closest connection to. But Charlie dutifully hauled himself out of the Ziffs' sedan and walked me up the brick path that led to my family's front door.

"This was fun," Charlie said as I slid my key into the lock. "Hey, I'll see you around school."

"Right . . . see you." I gave Charlie a smile, and he bent forward to give me a kiss on the cheek.

I slipped into the house and closed the door behind me. This night had been nothing like what I had expected. A week ago, if someone had told me that Charlie Simpson would be giving me a kiss on the cheek, I would have said that it was more likely that I would win a Lotto jackpot.

Now it had happened. And I felt let down. I didn't even care that Charlie hadn't asked me for another date. I was just glad to be inside my house, minutes away from scrubbing off my makeup and changing into a pair of soft cotton pajamas.

I walked into the den, where my parents were watching an A&E mystery classic. "I'm home," I announced.

My mom smiled. "Did you have fun, honey?"

I shrugged. "It was . . . interesting."

"We want to hear all about it in the morning," Dad added. "But we won't make you give us a full debriefing until you've had a chance to sort out your thoughts."

I laughed. My parents had never debriefed me in my life. Then again, I had never gone out on a double date on a Saturday night (or any night, for that matter) before. This day was definitely one for the record books. Plain Jane Smith had gone out with one of the most popular guys at Union High—and lived to tell the tale. There was only one problem. There wasn't much of a tale. No sordid details. No giggled confessions or wistful glances. It was just . . . a date.

131

Upstairs, I took off my new dress and carefully hung it up in my closet. I was getting more depressed by the minute now that I was alone with my thoughts. But why? I had accomplished one of my major goals tonight. I had gone out with Charlie, and I hadn't made a complete fool of myself. I even had the feeling that if I had tried just a little bit harder, I could have obtained that ever elusive second date.

"What's eating at you, Janie?" I asked myself, pulling on my favorite pair of pajamas. "Why are you so down in the dumps?"

But I knew why I felt so low. The answer had been staring me right in the face, almost since the moment that I opened the door and found myself face-to-face with the guy of my dreams. For the first time I had realized, somewhere deep inside, that my crush on Charlie had been totally superficial. It had been stupid, and childish, and based on nothing but a pair of bright blue eyes and a winning smile.

*It's all been meaningless,* I realized, pacing back and forth across my room. I had spent four years fantasizing about Charlie, but there hadn't been any *real* basis for my infatuation. Sure, he had been nice to me one time at a skating rink. But so what?

The truth was undeniable. My quest to transform myself into the kind of girl that Charlie would go for had been superficial—based on hair and makeup rather than any personality deficiency I might have had. And my crush had been equally superficial. I had fallen for Charlie because he had a great smile and broad shoulders.

But I had never really known him. I had never had a single real conversation with him—at least, not before tonight. I'd liked him because he was cute, and popular, and dazzling. Not because we had anything in common or found the same things funny or believed in the same causes.

*Basically I've had a crush on a celebrity,* I thought. I might as well have spent my time dreaming about Brad Pitt. Charlie was a face and a name to me—not a real, living, breathing person. How meaningless!

I charged into my bathroom, anxious to scrub away the seven layers of makeup on my face. The lather of the soap felt good in my hands and even better on my face. I massaged the soap into my skin, making it tingle.

How could I have been so stupid? It had taken me all this time to realize that what I felt for Charlie had no more substance than cotton candy. I had moped and mooned and pined for all this time . . . for absolutely no reason. I, Jane Smith, thought by some to be the smartest girl in school, had attached enormous importance to something (or, in this case, someone) that turned out to be totally unimportant.

I turned on the cold water tap and doused my cheeks, forehead, chin—sort of a metaphorical slap in the face. Now maybe I could see my life clearly and not through the gauze of my desperate attempt to "fit in."

At least one truth was already emerging from the fog. There was a real reason why I couldn't stop thinking about Max . . . couldn't stop dreaming about him. I *knew* Max. He was a real person, with whom I'd shared real conversations and real laughter. We had gotten to know each other in a way that I had never known another guy before.

As I was patting my face dry with a fresh towel, the phone on my nightstand rang. *It's got to be Nicole,* I guessed. Christy never called after ten o'clock.

"Hello," I answered, preparing myself for the half-hour grill session that would inevitably ensue.

"Hey, I hope you're not asleep yet." The voice didn't belong to Nicole. It was Max.

I placed my hand over my heart, willing it to stop beating so wildly within my chest. My blood pressure felt like it had risen astronomically during the last two seconds.

"Hi, Max. No . . . uh, I'm not asleep yet." *And now that you've called, it will probably be another three hours before I wind down enough to close my eyes,* I added silently.

"I just couldn't wait until Monday to hear what you thought about the date," Max told me. "Was it everything you had hoped it would be?"

I thought about lying and saying, yes, the date was beyond my wildest dreams. But what was the point? Charlie and I, as a couple, were never going to happen.

"I had a great time . . . but to tell you the truth, I don't think the date part between Charlie and me went that well."

"I know Charlie was being totally obnoxious, but hey, maybe he was nervous. He's probably never been out with a girl as cool and smart as you are."

I smiled. Leave it to Max to say something totally nice at exactly the right moment. He always came through.

"There's nothing wrong with Charlie," I assured him. "But—well, I don't think we really clicked the way I had hoped we would."

"You didn't?" Max didn't sound as disappointed as I thought he would. Probably because Charlie had already told him on the drive home that he never wanted to see me again.

"I think it would be best if we forget the whole thing," I suggested to Max. "Charlie, the transformation, all of it. I mean, your term papers will be finished, right on schedule . . . but . . . let's just leave it at that."

"No!" Max burst out. "We have to give it another shot!"

"Max—," I started, intending to tell him that I was happy with the progress I had made but that I thought I would be okay on my own from here on out.

"Things were just a little off tonight," he interrupted. "There was a weird vibe in the air. I think . . . I think there was just too much pressure on all of us—especially you." He paused. "But I'll think of something to fix it. I swear!"

I closed my eyes and sank into my pillows. More than anything, I wished I could tell Max that Charlie wasn't the one I wanted to go out with. I wished I could open up my heart and tell Max that I had fallen for *him*—and for all of the right reasons.

*The transformation was superficial and fake and has nothing to do with why someone should go for me,* I wanted to shout into the telephone.

But I couldn't. A relationship between Max and me was an impossibility. He was in love with Shana, and that wasn't going to change. That much was obvious from the way they kept kissing each other during dinner.

"Come on, Janie," Max urged. "Tell me you'll give Charlie another try. Please."

I bit my lip. I couldn't say no. Not to Max. He had done so much for me, and he was so determined to help me that I didn't have the heart to disappoint him. I would have felt terrible if he thought I was giving up on him in any way.

"One more shot," I agreed finally. "But if things don't work out with Charlie and me, I'll live. Really."

On the other end of the phone Max breathed a huge sigh of relief. "You won't be sorry, Jane. I know what I'm doing."

I almost felt like laughing. Max might know what *he* was doing. But I had no idea what *I* was doing. . . .

# Fifteen

## Jane

IGLANCED IN the girls' bathroom mirror on
Monday morning, debating whether or not to
apply another coat of lipstick. Last Friday, I would
have seized any opportunity to ensure that my
makeup was picture-perfect. Today . . . I didn't care
all that much. Besides, I didn't really like the lipstick I had bought—it tasted bad.

"Hey, Jane," Shana greeted me, breezing into
the bathroom, brush and makeup bag already in
hand. "I need to do a quick repair job." She gave
me a pointed look. "And so do you."

"Hi, Shana." Dutifully I pulled the tube of lipstick out of my backpack. I couldn't very well tell
Shana that after all of her hard work, I had decided
that I was okay with looking more or less the way I
had for the last four years.

"So . . . was Saturday night the best evening of your life—or what?" Shana inquired, dabbing concealer onto the nonexistent zits on her face.

"Uh . . ." How to answer that question? In some ways Saturday night *had* been great.

I had finally seen the truth, liberating myself from the pathetic crush that had dominated my waking hours for as long as I could remember. And I had also realized, at long last, that a person was more than a hairstyle, gleaming white teeth, and the right attitude.

But the date had also been horrible—and not just because my Charlie bubble had been burst. Now that I had realized what I *really* wanted— Max—the fact that I couldn't have him was more painful than anything I had experienced regarding Charlie. Of course, that particular piece of information was the *last* thing I would ever share with Shana.

"Charlie is, like, the funniest person I have ever met," Shana continued. She had moved on to powder, carefully dusting her face, then blotting with some kind of cotton pad. "He *totally* cracks me up."

"Yeah . . . he's really funny." Actually, I didn't have much of an opinion on whether or not Charlie was witty. I had spent the majority of the evening sneaking glances at Max—not appreciating Charlie's particular brand of humor.

"I don't know *what* was wrong with Max that night," Shana went on. "He was so uptight. I've never seen him act so . . . lame."

"Lame?" I asked, my voice a tiny squeak. "I didn't think Max was being lame."

Shana rolled her eyes—not an easy feat in the midst of applying a fresh coat of black mascara. "Sometimes Max is just so not fun. He's lucky that he's so cute—otherwise I wouldn't stick around for the bad times as well as the good ones."

I couldn't believe Shana felt this way. She had to appreciate Max for more than his dark hair and entrancing hazel-with-gold-flecks eyes. Didn't she feel like the luckiest girl in the world to be dating a guy who was so intelligent and sensitive and interesting and funny and . . . I had to stop myself. I couldn't think about Max like that. It was wrong, wrong, wrong.

Sure, any girl in her right mind would love the way Max *looked*. But that wasn't the most important thing about him—far from it. Appearance was . . . well, just that. *Appearance*. It didn't have anything to do with what was inside.

I had learned that much for myself—Saturday night. Which was why, unlike Shana, I would be spending prom night home alone, with a bag of Ruffles and an expensive aromatherapy kit.

Of course, it had taken me four years to learn the lesson. I couldn't blame Shana for not having the exact same epiphany I'd had.

"Hey, maybe you'll get lucky with Charlie," Shana said, her tone a combination of condescending and encouraging. "There's always a chance he'll ask you out again."

I didn't bother to tell Shana that I didn't think I *cared* whether or not Charlie asked me for another date. She wouldn't understand. Just like she didn't understand a lot of things—like Max's amazing personality. . . .

The last thing on my mind as I walked into Mr. Atkison's class was English literature. I was about to see Charlie—and Max. Since late Saturday night I had been wondering how I would feel when I saw Charlie again. Maybe when we were in class—where my crush had developed into a four-year-long obsession—I would rediscover the magic. Maybe.

I walked into the classroom, scanning the desks. Almost immediately my eyes fell on Charlie. He was unwrapping a package of frosted Pop-Tarts to go with the small carton of chocolate milk on the top of his desk.

He glanced up and caught my eye. "Hey," he greeted me. Then he turned back to the foil wrapper.

"Hey." I continued past his desk and took a seat in the back of the classroom.

Max was still nowhere in sight, so I decided to use the last few moments before the bell rang to dissect my reaction to Charlie. I closed my eyes, tuning out the sounds of scraping chairs, laughter, and rustling notebook pages.

I had seen Charlie. He had nodded and said hi. I had nodded and said hi. And that was it. There had been no lingering anxiety. My palms hadn't been sweaty, and my heart hadn't raced. I had felt neither happy that he said hello nor *unhappy* that *all* he said was hello.

The truth was clear. I felt nothing for Charlie Simpson. Nada. Zip. Nil. Absolutely, positively, definitely *nothing*. My crush was over. The spark was officially, unequivocally dead.

It was as if a huge weight had been lifted from my shoulders. I was free! From now on I could roam the corridors of Union High without feeling compelled to be vigilant about searching for a Charlie sighting. I would no longer have a sick knot in the pit of my stomach when I heard a rumor that Charlie had been spotted making out with one of the cheerleaders under the football-stadium bleachers.

Unfortunately I still felt like a fool for harboring such a meaningless crush for so long. Who knew what interesting and dynamic thoughts I might have had during the time I had spent fantasizing about Charlie? Maybe I could even have met someone—someone like Max—if I hadn't been longing for a guy I didn't even know.

I opened my eyes just as Max was entering the classroom. Zing. Zing. Every nerve in my body felt charged with electricity as my eyes followed Max's easy gait.

*Don't think about Max like that,* I ordered myself. I had to put him out of my mind completely— at least as anything more than a good friend. I tore my gaze away and stared at my notebook. A moment later I felt Max looking at me, but I didn't glance up. If it's true that a person's eyes are the windows to her soul, I didn't want Max to look into mine and see how I really felt.

I waited for everyone else to file out of the classroom before I finally picked up my backpack and headed for my next class. I didn't want to talk to Max now—I wasn't ready.

"Hey, slowpoke, what took you so long?" I felt Max's hand on my arm before I registered his voice.

I stopped short, just outside the classroom door. "Oh, hi, Max. I was just, uh, making sure I had my calculator for calculus."

Max pulled me out of the throng of students crowding the hallway. "I've got a plan."

"A plan?" I repeated back to him, trying in vain to ignore the way his hand on my arm had sent little shivers up and down my spine.

Max nodded. "Jason Frango is having a party on Friday night. Charlie is going to be there— and so are you."

I frowned. A month ago, even a week ago, I would have been jumping up and down at having received an actual invitation to an actual party where there would be actual cool people. But now . . . Well, the prospect of watching Max and Shana slow dancing and making out wasn't the first thing on my list of fun weekend activities.

"I barely even know Jason. I don't think he'd want me at his party." It wasn't the real reason I didn't want to go, but it was true.

Max gave me the head shake. "No way, Janie.

You're not getting out of this." His gaze was piercing, and I could barely breathe. "You promised to give you and Charlie one more shot, and Friday night is the perfect opportunity. I'm sure this time you two will totally click."

"Charlie barely bothered to say hi to me in English class," I pointed out. "I really don't think he's interested."

"How can he *not* fall for you?" Max wondered aloud. "You're the coolest chick I know. . . . I mean, uh, aside from Shana, of course."

Of course. I wasn't likely to forget that fact! "Max, I really appreciate all you've done." I was going to say a firm no to the party. I really was. But looking into Max's eyes, I simply couldn't let him down. "And I'd like to go to the party. It's a great idea."

He nodded. "Good. Now, there's one more thing we need to talk about."

His tone had changed—it was all business. My heart sort of shriveled as I remembered the real reason Max had been hanging out with me at all. He valued me, all right—but only because I was the one who was writing his term papers.

"I've told you five times that your papers will be done, typed, and spell checked right on time," I informed him, sounding a little testy.

"Listen, Jane, I've been doing a lot of thinking." He paused, shuffling his feet and staring at the floor. "Um, I don't want you to write the papers. It's just not right. I'm going to do them myself."

I had to put my hand over my mouth to keep

my jaw from dropping to the ground. Was Max saying what I thought he was saying? After all he had gone through, he wasn't even going to bear the fruits (in the form of twenty pages of carefully written exposition) of his labors?

"Max, I don't know what to say. I mean, we had a deal. . . ."

He grinned. "Let's call our deal to a close—officially. I think we both got a lot out of it, but it's time to call it quits."

Call it quits. No more Max and Jane, working together to make our lives better. We wouldn't be spending any more afternoons together in the library, quietly researching Max's history term paper. Our business was finished.

"If that's what you want, Max, then I'll give you the note cards I've made. You can go from here."

"Thanks, Jane. For everything." His tone had a good-bye in it.

"If the deal is off, it's off," I told him. "We can just forget about Friday night and the party and Charlie—"

"No way!" Max interrupted. "Friday night is on the house. You *are* going to be there!"

I watched Max take off down the hall, feeling more confused than ever. Max had agreed to help me—and he wasn't going to get anything out of it. That meant . . . Well, it meant that we were friends. Max *really* wanted Charlie to fall for me—and not just because he felt obligated.

Even as our partnership was drawing to a close, I felt closer to Max than ever. Closer—and more in love.

# Sixteen

## Jane

"**D**O EITHER OF you want to join me for a John Travolta movie marathon this weekend?" Christy asked Nicole and me at lunch on Thursday. "We can start with the seventies and *Saturday Night Fever* and keep right on going through the nineties."

"Count me in," Nicole answered. "As long as you promise to leave *Phenomenon* out of the lineup. Once was enough."

"Deal," Christy said. She turned to me. "So, Jane, any special Travolta requests? *Broken Arrow*? *Get Shorty*? The seminal classic, *Perfect*?"

"I don't know if I can join you guys for the fest," I said, opening a can of Dr Pepper. "I, uh, might have plans."

I had been hoping to avoid this conversation. So

far, I hadn't mentioned Jason's party to either Nicole or Christy because I still wasn't totally committed to going. And I knew that discussing the matter would only stir all of the confusing emotions I had been experiencing all week.

"What gives?" Nicole demanded. "You've been acting weird all week."

"It's Max," I told them. "Actually, it's Charlie. No, it's Max *and* Charlie." Jeez. I was confusing *myself.*

"You had better start from the beginning," Christy told me. "This sounds complicated."

In the simplest possible terms I explained to my friends that my feelings for Charlie had changed. I had simply lost interest in the guy who had been my obsession for all of high school.

"But Max is insisting that I go to a party at Jason Frango's on Friday night. He's positive that Charlie and I will hit it off this time around."

"Maybe you will," Christy said hopefully. "I mean, crazier things have happened."

I shook my head sadly. "Even if Charlie was interested, there's no way I'd rekindle my crush." I paused. "I'm . . . in love with somebody else."

Phew. It was the first time I'd allowed myself to *think* those words, much less say them aloud. I felt exhilarated and sick all at the same time.

"I think we have a tiny inkling who," Nicole said with a smile, and Christy nodded.

I glanced up at both of them in surprise. My best friends had known it even before I did. I was the only person I was keeping it a secret from.

"That's so great!" Christy said, then paused. "Uh, is it great?"

"It's terrible." I had been thinking about nothing but Max, Charlie, and the party all week. And any way I examined the situation, I came out a big, fat loser. "First of all, Max already has a girlfriend he's totally in love with. Second, Shana has become a friend of mine. Third, even if Shana wasn't in the picture, I doubt that Max would ever view me as more than a buddy."

Nicole frowned. "Max seems like a really nice guy, but I don't know how you can consider Shana Stevens to be a friend. Her favorite pastime is ragging on people like us."

"She's really not like that," I assured my friends. "She's been so nice to me. Shana even offered to help me get ready for the party Friday night so I would have a better chance with Charlie."

"If you don't want to go to the party, why did you tell Max you would?" Christy asked.

I sighed. "He was just so sweet about wanting me to have another shot with Charlie. . . . I couldn't say no."

Nicole snapped her fingers. "Hey, there is a bright side to this!" she announced.

"What?" I had been searching for a bright side all week, and I hadn't found one.

"If you go to the party," Nicole began in a cheery voice, "and Charlie ends up asking you to the prom . . . Well, there are worse things in the world than going to the dance with a gorgeous guy you've fancied yourself in love with for your entire high-school career. Even if you don't still have a crush on him, it would be fun."

"And," Christy added, "if there's zero chemistry with you and Charlie and he *doesn't* ask you to the prom, then at least you'll get to spend a little more time around Max."

They were right. Going to the prom had been one of my lifelong dreams. And if I couldn't go with the guy of my real dreams, that didn't mean I couldn't go with someone else. If that person turned out to be Charlie Simpson, so much the better. Hey, at least I'd have a great photo of me in a prom dress with one of the hottest guys at Union High.

*And if Charlie doesn't ask me . . . no harm done.* I had managed to hang out around Max and Shana while they were making out before. Once more wouldn't kill me.

"I'll go!" I told my friends. "And I'll give Charlie everything I've got—for old times' sake."

It wasn't as if anything *bad* would come of me going to Jason Frango's party. At the very least I would get to see how the other half lived. *Who knows?* I thought. *Maybe I'll even have a good time.*

"Tonight is going to be a total blast," Shana chirped, twirling around her bedroom in a new skirt. "Jason's parents are out of town for, like, a week, so it's going to be a total rager."

"Cool." I pictured drunk jocks swinging from chandeliers while their dates did striptease acts on the dining-room table. Was I getting in over my head? Would cops show up?

This whole night was shaping up to be totally surreal. I, not-so-plain Jane Smith, was hanging out with Shana Stevens in her bedroom—which was awe inspiring in and of itself. Pink wall-to-wall carpet. Pink curtains. Pink walls. A four-poster bed with a white comforter and pink pillows. I felt like I was visiting a Barbie Dream House.

"So what are you wearing tonight?" Shana asked. She slipped on a pair of high-heeled sandals and looked at herself in the mirror that took up an entire wall of her bedroom.

I looked down at myself. "Uh . . . this." Flowered, knee-length miniskirt, white T-shirt, white sandals. Shana had *liked* the outfit when she picked it out for me at the mall last weekend.

"Oh. Well, you look nice." She studied me from head to toe, and I didn't need to be a rocket scientist to realize that she wasn't blown away by what she saw.

"But?" I was starting to panic. I hadn't brought anything else to wear, but I would feel totally self-conscious walking into her crowd's party in an ensemble that Shana, queen of fashion, didn't approve.

"What you're wearing would be perfect for school—or an afternoon baseball game. But it's not really right for Jason's party . . . especially if you want to get Charlie's attention."

"Oh." I looked at myself in Shana's mirror. I thought I looked pretty good, but what did I know? Shana was the expert.

"You probably don't know this, Jane, but Charlie has a major thing for leather." Shana's voice was low and conspiratorial, as if she were revealing the identity of Deep Throat.

"Leather?" I squeaked. I had an image of myself dressed up in a red leather bustier, carrying a whip and a chain.

Shana nodded. She opened the door of her huge walk-in closet and pulled out the smallest skirt I had ever seen—at least, I *thought* it was a skirt. It could have been a halter top. It was black leather, and it looked like something Cher would have worn in the 1980s.

"This baby will drive Charlie wild," Shana declared. "*Trust* me."

I gulped. Could I really walk into a crowded room wearing that . . . garment? I had gained a certain measure of self-confidence, but donning a leather micromini was testing the limit.

Nonetheless, I obediently put on the skirt, along with a tight, bright red tank top that Shana pulled out of the bottom drawer of her dresser. At Shana's urging, I added a pair of black stilettos.

"I don't know, Shana. . . . It's not really me." I pivoted in front of the mirror. This outfit was appropriate for an MTV music video, but I felt downright foolish.

"Charlie will love it," Shana assured me. "He'll go totally wild when he sees this side of you."

I bit my lip. So far, Shana hadn't steered me wrong. Maybe this outfit wasn't Max's ideal, but he wasn't the one I was trying to impress. A prom date was what I was after—which meant Charlie. And if I was going to do this flirting thing, I might as well do it right.

"I'll wear it," I announced. "Thanks, Shana."

She grinned. "My pleasure—believe me."

I walked back and forth across the carpet, trying to get the hang of those superhigh heels. Now I knew how those Olympic gymnasts felt when they were performing on the balance beam in front of a stadium full of people.

Shana sifted through her jewelry box, looking for the perfect accessories to go with her new outfit. "So, Jane, what's your plan tonight?"

I teetered, then caught myself on one of the bedposts. "Plan?"

"With Charlie," she said, inserting a small diamond stud into her ear. "How are you going to get him to fall head over heels for you?"

"I, uh, don't know. . . ." Up until now, I had intended to be myself, plus a little mindless chitchat, and hope for the best.

"Can I give you a little friendly advice, Jane?" Shana asked, her voice suddenly serious.

"Of course." I wasn't about to turn down pearls of wisdom from the girl who had managed to snare the heart of the guy of my dreams. Clearly she knew something—lots of things—that I didn't.

"You were too nice to Charlie last Saturday night," Shana informed me. "You know . . . too eager to please."

"I was?" I had thought the opposite was true. As soon as I had abandoned conversation that had centered around *my* interests and focused instead on those subjects that Charlie liked, he seemed to perk up.

"Yep." Shana took her blush brush and added another layer of color to my cheeks. "See, Jane, Charlie loves nothing more than to be insulted by a girl. You've got to bait him."

Huh. This was a form of flirting that was entirely new to me. Then again, Charlie *had* seemed to enjoy his vaguely insulting banter with our big-busted waitress. Maybe Shana was making sense.

"Are you sure, Shana?" I asked. "I don't have a lot of experience with insulting popular, gorgeous jocks."

Shana gave me a warm, encouraging smile. "Jane, you're the smartest girl in school. I *know* you can do this."

I nodded. *What do I have to lose?* I asked myself. It wasn't as if I'd had a lot of luck with Charlie going about things *my* way. And Shana knew Charlie a hundred times better than I did. If she said this was the way to go, well, then, this *was* the way to go.

I didn't have a lot of confidence in my ability to trade funny insults with a hot guy, but I might as well go for it. Even if that meant acting totally outside the normal realm of my personality.

*I'll do my best,* I resolved. At the very least, I would try to make Shana—and Max—proud. And maybe, just maybe, I would end the night with an invitation to the prom. Like Nicole had said, worse things had happened . . . right?

# Seventeen

## Max

ON FRIDAY NIGHT I circled what Jason had jokingly referred to as the hors d'oeuvre table. It consisted of a folding-card table laden with unopened bags of potato chips, jars of salsa, and tins of room-temperature nacho cheese.

I opened a bag of Ruffles and stuffed a couple into my mouth. But as I was chewing, I realized that I had absolutely no appetite. The potato chips made my stomach churn. *What's wrong with me?* I wondered.

Usually I was hungry twenty-four hours a day. But all week I had been feeling sort of queasy. And a couple of nights when I had been hanging out with Shana, I had gotten splitting headaches. It was almost as if my body was trying to tell me something . . . but I didn't know what.

"Yo, Max, where's the squeeze?" Jim Grange

called from the other side of the living room. "Did she dump you or what?"

I rolled my eyes. The guys I hung out with had their good points, but tact wasn't among them. "Shana's meeting me here," I informed Jim. "And she's bringing Jane Smith with her."

Jim nodded. "Cute chick. Nice legs." He paused. "A little too brainy, though. She probably spends most nights reading Plato or learning a foreign language."

I didn't respond. Why bother? I knew how cool Jane was. And that was all that mattered. Besides, I had a feeling that after tonight, a lot more people were going to realize how amazing Jane really was.

I left Jason standing next to the chips table and headed for the kitchen. I needed ginger ale. Or maybe some seltzer water. Anything to calm my stomach.

"Hey, Ziff, you ready to get wild?" Charlie asked as I entered the kitchen. He was mixing a batch of infamous party punch.

"Uh . . . yeah. Sure." I grabbed a 7UP from the fridge and walked out.

The sight of Charlie had made me feel worse than ever. Why? We were friends. Good friends. But I found myself, inexplicably, hating his guts.

Suddenly I wished I hadn't encouraged Shana when she suggested that she help Jane get ready for tonight. Shana had said she wanted Jane to get her "special treatment." At the time the extra "tutor" session had seemed like an awesome idea.

I remembered Shana's promise. *Max, you have*

*my word that tonight there's no way Charlie will fail to notice Jane. I'll make sure of that.*

I had told Shana that I was hoping tonight would be *the* night for Jane and Charlie. But my gut was telling me something different. The truth was that I dreaded the idea of Charlie and Jane hooking up tonight. I hated to think of them making out in some dark room of Jason's house.

I took a sip of the 7UP and tried to push the image of Charlie holding Jane close out of my mind. But it was quickly replaced by another. Prom night. What if Charlie really *did* ask Jane to the prom?

I knew for a fact that he still hadn't decided who he was going to invite. Charlie had told me at practice just the other day that he was tired of all the girls we hung out with. He had said he wanted some "fresh blood."

Ugh. I pictured Jane in some slinky, shiny, strapless dress. She was slow dancing with Charlie, and he was pulling her closer and closer as they swayed to some cheesy eighties tune. Jane gazed up at her dream guy, batting her eyelashes and giggling. *Yuck!*

I paced up and down the Frangos' front hallway, holding the cold can of soda to my damp forehead. What really got to me was Jane's part in all of this. How was it possible that she had fallen for a guy like Charlie? I was disappointed in her. Profoundly disappointed that her taste would be so, well, predictable.

Didn't she realize that Charlie was just like all of the other so-so guys at Union High? I expected more from Jane. Worst of all, I felt like I didn't know her as well as I thought I did. Was she really the person I thought she was?

Yes, I had set out to change Jane. But in truth, I felt like *she* had changed *me*. Jane had made me realize how superficial my whole world was. I wasn't thrilled to see, at this point, that Jane's transformation had been a success.

I had done exactly what Jane asked—turned her, at least on the surface, into the kind of girl that I would go for. A girl just like Shana. *And that's the problem,* I thought.

Jane had made me realize, unintentionally, that Shana cared more about my letterman's jacket than she did about *me*. As for myself . . . Did I really care about *her?* Or did I just like her because she was gorgeous and popular and made the other guys jealous of me for having her as my girlfriend?

Yes, I liked Shana. But my emotions toward her were totally different from my feelings toward Jane. With Jane, I could be myself. With Jane, I laughed, debated, *talked.* I was always thrilled to see Jane come into a room, and I was always sorry to see her leave.

*Oh, man . . .* My stomach dropped into my feet as I realized what I must have known in my heart of hearts for a while now. *I'm in love with Jane!* At some point, between teaching her how to act casually around guys and arguing with her over opera, I had fallen head over heels in love with Jane Smith.

As soon as I realized the truth, my heart sank.

Jane had made it totally clear that she wanted Charlie—the guy she was planning to win over this very night, at this very party, in this very living room.

*It's hopeless,* I thought. *Jane will never be mine . . . especially after tonight.*

Miles Evans and John Gold appeared in the hallway. "Hey, Max!" Miles called. "Want to check out Jason's new Sega game before all the girls get here?"

"Where is it?" I asked. I'm not really the video-game type—but I was searching for anything to take my mind off Jane and Charlie.

"Upstairs," John informed me. "In Jason's room."

"Count me in." I headed up the front stairs two at a time.

Anything was better than watching Jane enter the party and start making her moves on Charlie. If I had to watch them flirting with each other, I might literally lose my mind. My head would explode, and there would be brain matter all over the Frangos' white plush wall-to-wall carpet. That would be bad. Very, very bad.

With any luck at all, I could stay upstairs all night, avoiding Jane, avoiding Charlie, and avoiding Shana. Hey, maybe I could even avoid the pathetic mess my *life* had become. . . .

# Eighteen

## Jane

BY THE TIME Shana and I pulled up in front of Jason Frango's house in her white Cabrio convertible, the street was lined with cars. I saw Max's dad's car parked in the driveway and breathed a sigh of relief. Seeing Max would be painful, but at least I knew that I would have someone to talk to if I turned out to be a party flop.

"Good. We're fashionably late." Shana jerked on the parking brake. "I *always* make an entrance. And tonight—so will you."

"Can't wait." I got out of the car, mentally preparing myself to walk into a house full of cool kids wearing a skirt so short it might as well have been a belt. This wasn't going to be easy.

I tailed Shana up the front walk with a moderate degree of success (one trip, one twisted ankle).

Shana didn't bother to ring the doorbell. With a measure of confidence I could only dream of, she threw open the front door and strode in. I followed, wishing in a major way that I at least had a sweater to drape over my bare shoulders.

"Hi, Shana!" Madison sang out as soon as we entered.

Shana sent her friend a smile, then turned to me. "Good luck, Jane. I'll be watching from the sidelines."

Uh-oh. We weren't ten seconds into the party, and already I had been abandoned. At least for now. *Be strong,* I ordered myself. I was armed with all of my new knowledge. There was no reason I couldn't take this party by storm . . . or at least blend into the crowd.

I edged around the perimeter of the living room, scanning for Max. Unfortunately he was nowhere in sight. *Maybe that's for the best,* I decided. As long as Max was around, I was going to have a tough time staying focused on my target—Charlie.

By the time I reached the far end of the living room, I realized that I wasn't quite as inconspicuous as I had thought I was. Several people were not only *glancing* at me—they were *staring.*

I backed up against the wall, wanting to hide. Why had I let Shana talk me into wearing this outfit? It was . . . outrageous. I had no business baring this much of my skin to a viewing public. It was practically indecent!

"Hey, Jane!" Jason called from the kitchen. "There's punch in here if you want some."

"Uh . . . thanks." Huh. Maybe I was imagining

159

the stares. Jason hadn't looked at me as if I were a stripper—he had merely been friendly.

*They're probably just not used to my new look,* I decided. The fact that everyone was doing a double take when they saw me didn't mean I looked *bad.* It meant just the opposite. Shana herself had assured me that I looked amazing. And she was the most fashion-conscious—and fashion-critical—person I had ever met.

*And this is what Charlie likes,* I reminded myself. *That's what matters.* I sighed. *For tonight anyway.*

Despite the fact that I kept telling myself I was here to put the moves on Charlie, I hadn't stopped searching the crowded room for Max's face. Every time my eyes fell on a guy with dark, curly hair, my heart skipped a beat. But so far, nothing. Didn't he even care enough to say hello?

Man. This whole night was shaping up to be a disaster. Max didn't like me. And I was too shy to go up to Charlie and start a conversation. Besides, if this was the outfit I had to wear to get Charlie's attention at a party, what would he expect me to wear to the prom as his date? I had a flash of myself in a short, metallic, mesh dress. Yikes! Not a pretty picture.

*I'll just tell Shana that if this is what Charlie likes, then, well, this isn't who I am.* Why go through the motions of attracting a guy under false pretenses? Was it even fair? Besides, if I bowed out of this whole charade, then I could go home—and be off the hook. I could get into bed and read a book, or do a crossword puzzle, or catch up on the piles of homework that I had been neglecting.

Suddenly Shana loomed at my side. And she didn't look happy. "Jane, why are you standing over here in the corner?" she demanded. "You're supposed to be mingling—with Charlie."

"Shana, I . . ." My voice trailed off as Nicole's and Christy's words echoed in my brain.

*You've got nothing to lose. Hey, maybe you'll fulfill your lifelong dream and get to go to the prom. You've got nothing to lose.* Nicole and Christy were right. I was here—I might as well go for it. Worst-case scenario, Charlie ignored me. Then I could slip quietly out of the party, knowing that I had done my best.

"I've just been trying to figure out what to say," I told Shana. "But I'll go over there. Right now."

Steeling myself, I threw back my shoulders, stuck out my breasts, and sauntered (or staggered) toward Charlie. He was standing with a group of football players, and they were all laughing hysterically as one of them crushed an empty can of root beer against his forehead. *Not an easy group to infiltrate,* I thought warily.

I stopped right next to Charlie. "Hi!" I exclaimed, heralding my presence in the only way I knew how.

Charlie turned. "Hey, Jane." He raised his eyebrows. "You're looking . . . good."

"Thanks." I wanted to say something else, but I was at a loss. So I just stood there with a stupid smile on my face.

Charlie turned back to his friends. Oops. I had

let my first opportunity pass right by. I needed to make a splash, and I needed to do it fast. Otherwise I was going to lose my nerve, not to mention my interest, altogether. I tuned back into the conversation and realized that Charlie was in the middle of telling a story.

Shana's advice ran through my brain like a ticker tape. She had told me to be aggressive. She had said Charlie liked to be baited and taunted by a girl. If I wanted to get his attention, I really had to be *out* there.

". . . So I told the guy to *bite me,* and then I walked off!" Charlie finished.

As the rest of the guys laughed, I planted myself directly in front of Charlie's line of vision. *Ready, set, go.*

"Is being a dumb jock as painful as it looks?" I asked sweetly, batting my eyelashes à la Olga the Waitress.

Charlie's mouth dropped open. "Gee, Jane, I've never really thought about it," he answered. "Let me get back to you on that one."

"Sure thing," I said. "I'll be waiting with bated breath for your insightful, compelling answer."

"Okay . . ." Charlie gave me a strange look, then turned back to his friends again.

This little performance wasn't going all that well. If anything, Charlie seemed annoyed. I glanced over at Shana, who was standing several feet away with Rose and Madison. She flashed me a thumbs-up and an encouraging smile.

For a few moments I was silent, smiling and nodding along with the general flow of conversation.

When there was a lull, I decided to jump in again.

"Charlie, did you know that the number of muscles a guy has are in indirect proportion to the size of his brain . . . among other things?"

Charlie stared at me with a confused look on his face. Clearly I had stumped him. "Do you need me to explain what 'indirect proportion' means?" I asked, lowering my voice in what I hoped was a sultry, seductive manner.

Charlie ran a hand through his hair, gazing at me through hooded eyes. His expression was blank. "Jane—"

"Careful," I admonished. "You might mess up the pound of gel in your hair." I was really on a roll now. The insults were sliding off my tongue with no effort at all.

I felt like I was having an out-of-body experience. This wasn't Jane Smith talking. It was some foreign being who had no sense of tact, decency, or restraint. In a weird way, I felt liberated. But I also felt . . . fake.

"And another thing—" I stopped midsentence, crashing back to reality.

The music had stopped. And everyone in the room was looking at me. Not just looking. *Staring.* And not in a nice way. They seemed . . . horrified.

Charlie glared at me. "Hey, Shana!" he called. "Can you do something about your friend? She's totally pathetic." He laughed. "And she's too mean—even for me!"

★      ★      ★

*She's pathetic.* All of the blood drained from my face as Charlie's words registered. I felt like I was going to faint, or throw up, or both. *She's pathetic.* With every passing second my sense of horror increased exponentially.

*This isn't happening,* I told myself. *I'm having a nightmare.* Or maybe it was all a big misunderstanding. Maybe everybody staring at me with disgusted expressions on their faces was some kind of cool-kids' party ritual that Max and Shana had forgotten to warn me about.

I looked over at Shana, willing her to come to the rescue. But she didn't give me another thumbs-up. And she didn't rush to my side to explain to everyone that they had the wrong impression—that I was actually a totally cool person who everyone should make an effort to get to know.

*Shana is laughing,* I realized. She was laughing with her friends, and they were all pointing at me as if I were some piece of garbage on one of their pristine bedroom floors.

I was frozen to my spot, unable to move, to speak, to breathe. This was the worst moment of my life. And I was utterly powerless to do anything about it.

After what seemed like three lifetimes, but was probably only a few seconds, Shana broke away from Rose and Madison. She strolled to my side and led me away from Charlie and his friends.

"Jane, did you *really* think I was going to help make you popular?" she asked. Her beautiful smile had turned into an ugly sneer, and her eyes were shooting poisonous darts in my direction.

"I . . ." No words would come.

Shana laughed again. "I only agreed to help Max with his little 'lab experiment' to keep him happy," Shana informed me. "But as long as I had to do my good-girlfriend duties, I figured . . . hey, why not have some fun of my own?"

"You're . . ." I wanted to tell her that she was the lowest form of life. I wanted to tell Shana that she and her friends didn't deserve to be on the same planet as me, much less use me as a tool for their perverse kicks. But I couldn't speak.

"You see, Jane, my friend Rose has had her sights set on Charlie for a while now. There was no way I could help *you* snag the guy that my *real* friend wanted for herself." She smiled. "You understand that, don't you?"

Out of the corner of my eye I saw Max heading down the front stairs with a couple of guys trailing behind him. *Max.* Had he been in on this sick joke? Had he and Shana been laughing behind my back all along?

"Hey, Jane, no hard feelings," Shana chirped. "I didn't mean any harm."

*Get out!* From the deep recesses of my soul an inner voice spoke to me. *Get out now!*

I jerked away from Shana, pushing my way through the living room full of people. I kept my eyes fixed on the front door, determined not to cry right here, right now, where all of these horrible people could watch.

165

"Jane!" Max called out. "Janie, wait!"

I ignored Max. Like a girl possessed, I stumbled to the door. Still holding back my tears, I yanked open the door and sprinted into the dark night. I raced down the street, struggling to put as much distance between myself and that party as I could, as fast as I could.

"Jane . . ." Max's voice was fainter now. I was halfway down the block, and I kept on running.

I wouldn't stop until I was home, upstairs and safe in my own room. This had been the worst night of my life. In the space of half an hour my entire world had collapsed into a heap of ashes.

I had been humiliated, degraded, metaphorically spat upon. And it was all my fault. I had trusted the enemy. And now I was paying for it.

# Nineteen

## Jane

B Y THE TIME I reached the front door of my
house, I was sweating and my feet were covered with blisters from Shana's shoes. The walk had
numbed me, blocking out the image of Shana's
laughing face, of Charlie's angry glare.

But as soon as I entered our front hallway, I was
flooded with emotion. At last the tears flowed
freely down my face. I tore off the offending high
heels and threw them into the corner of our front-
hall closet. After I slammed the closet door shut, I
was aware of a deafening, overpowering silence.

*At least I have one thing to be grateful for,* I
thought. Mom and Dad had gone to a dinner party,
and they wouldn't be home for hours. By that time
I would be buried under my blankets, totally hid-
den from their well-meaning concern.

I used the last of my strength to sprint upstairs and into my room. I closed the door and leaned against it. I had thought I would feel better once I was back in my own room, with my own things. But I didn't. If anything, I felt worse.

Now that I wasn't running away from the scene of the crime, every grisly detail was playing over and over in my head. How could I have been such a fool? I had even *defended* Shana to Nicole and Christy, telling them that once I had gotten to know her, I had liked her. Stupid!

I had to get out of this ridiculous outfit. Now! I peeled off the leather miniskirt and stripped off the tank top. Then I rolled them both in a ball and stuffed them in the bottom of my trash can. If I'd had more guts, I would have burned them.

Wearing just my bra and underwear, I lurched into the bathroom. I turned the hot water on full blast, then scrubbed off every bit of the garish makeup Shana had painted my face with. Stupid! I had *known* I didn't look attractive with all that blue stuff around my eyes—unless one thought looking like a Las Vegas showgirl was a good thing. But I had let her dress me up like some kind of anti–Barbie doll anyway.

*Why?* I asked myself, staring into the mirror, as I had so many times in the past week. *Because you didn't think you were good enough,* I told my reflection. I had been willing to put all of *me* away in some imaginary closet just so that a group of shallow, self-involved people would think I was *somebody*.

I had brought tonight on myself. I had trusted Shana. I had trusted . . . Max. Fresh tears streamed down my face as I thought about Max. Had he known Shana was planning to humiliate me?

I pulled my hair back into a loose ponytail, thinking of Max. I couldn't believe that was true. I *knew* Max. He was my friend. Or was he? My entire world had turned upside down, and I felt like the truth was a lie and lies were the truth. Everything in my life had lost its meaning.

I walked to my dresser, taking deep breaths, willing myself to stop crying. Those people didn't deserve my tears. They weren't worth it. I opened the bottom drawer of my bureau and pulled out my favorite pair of faded blue jeans. I hadn't worn them since I had begun my transformation, and I experienced a wave of comfort as I slid the soft material over my body.

"That's more like it," I announced to an imaginary audience. "And to complete the ensemble, I will be donning a ratty old T-shirt." I grabbed my favorite one, a relic from my grandparents' pilgrimage to the Grand Canyon, and pulled it over my head.

I was me again. Plain Jane Smith, doer of homework, acer of tests, baby-sitter extraordinaire. From this moment forward I vowed to be one hundred percent myself, one hundred percent of the time. I had learned that anything else led to utter disaster.

I flopped onto my bed and put a pillow over my head. *You still have to go to school on Monday,* I reminded myself. Ugh. I could already hear the giggles, the snide comments. There would probably be a sign posted in the cafeteria: Plain Jane Smith—Loser of the Year.

All I had wanted was a date to my senior prom. Was that evil? Did wanting to be a part of things make me a pathetic, terrible person? Clearly the answer was yes. I had set out to upset the scales of popularity, breaking all rules of high-school social strata.

And my reward for making this one mistake was that I had been humiliated by the very crowd that I had been trying to be a part of. Even worse, I had been betrayed. Not to mention that I was heartbroken. I had found my own version of hell, and it consisted of Shana Stevens, Charlie Simpson, and Jason Frango's living room. And Max.

*Max. Max. Max.* We would never go bowling together again. There would be no more discussions about opera or movies or books. I would never make Max laugh again. Or see his eyes twinkling at me with that special light that made me feel excited, and faint, and warm all at the same time.

But Max wasn't the person I'd thought he was. There was no way a guy who loved Shana could be the right guy for me. It was obvious that his bright exterior hid something. Otherwise he never would have let this happen to me.

*But none of that matters,* I told myself. Who Max was or wasn't didn't concern me anymore. I never wanted to speak to him again.

I threw the pillow across my room and heaved

myself off the bed. I needed to listen to some music—at full volume—to drown out the images, the thoughts, the words that were torturing me. I headed toward my stereo, wiping away what I hoped were the last of my tears.

Staring at my CD collection, which included the new ones Max had suggested, nothing seemed right. Tori Amos—too soulful. Jewel—too romantic. Ricky Martin—too *male*. And opera was out. I wished I had some heavy metal that I could blast for all of the neighbors to hear.

*Ping.* "What . . . ?" I stood up straight and turned toward my bedroom windows.

I had heard something. Or had I? It was probably my imagination. I was overwrought, and now I was hallucinating the presence of some nefarious prowler. *Reality, Jane. We're dealing with reality only now.*

*Ping.* There it was again. The same noise. I walked slowly toward my window, unsure about what to expect. *Ping. Ping.* I had locked the front door. The police were only a 911 call away. I was safe—more or less.

My window was open. A small pebble missed the glass and fell onto the hardwood floor of my bedroom. I leaned out of the window and looked down into our front yard.

And I saw Max. He was holding a fistful of tiny rocks, and he was about to let another one fly.

"Jane!" he called. "Janie, we have to talk!"

Talk about nerve! Who did he think he was? I

couldn't believe he dared to speak to me, much less show up at my house. "Go away, Max!" I shouted. "I never want to talk to you again!"

He didn't move. "Jane, you *have* to let me come inside. Please."

I snorted. "You and your friends didn't have enough fun the first time around?" I asked. "You want to come inside and enjoy part two of the *Plain Jane Show*?"

"It's not like that, Janie. Please, let me explain."

"I've been *humiliated*, Max." I fought back a new batch of tears as I stared at his beautiful face. "I don't want to face you—or anyone else—ever again."

Max was shaking his head in a way that had become painfully familiar. "I'm begging you," he called. "Just give me five minutes, and then I swear I'll leave you alone."

I knew I should shut the window, turn up the music, and climb into bed. But I couldn't say no to Max. *Isn't that how I've gotten myself in all this trouble*? I thought ruefully. *I'll give him three minutes, and then it's good-bye forever,* I resolved.

"I'll come down," I told him. "But only because you begged."

The trip from my bedroom to the front door seemed to take forever. As much as I told myself that I hated Max, there was still a part of me that couldn't wait to see him face-to-face. *I really am pathetic,* I thought.

★　　★　　★

"So . . . talk, Max." We were standing in the foyer. I wasn't about to invite him to sit down and make himself comfortable

"Jane, I'm so sorry," Max began, wringing his hands. "I had no idea what Shana was up to. I swear."

I shrugged. "I'll get over it. You and your friends had your laughs, but I'm a stronger, better person than they'll ever be."

"Yes. You are." Max took a step forward. For a second I thought he was going to reach out and touch my arm . . . but he seemed to think better of it.

"Is that it?" I asked. "Are we done now?"

"No, we're not *done*," Max responded. "I want to tell you something. And when I'm done, if you tell me you hate me, I promise I'll never bother you again."

I sighed. I wanted to be able to turn off my feelings for Max like a water faucet. But it was impossible. Even now I knew that I was in love with him. And I couldn't shut him down . . . at least, not until he had said what he came to say.

"I'm listening," I said, this time with a little less frost in my tone. "Go on."

"I had no idea what was going on when I came downstairs at Jason's tonight. I knew you were upset, but I didn't really understand what had happened." He took a deep breath, seeming to search for the right words. "After you left, I found out what Shana had done."

173

"And?" I believed Max that he hadn't known what Shana was planning. Deep down, I didn't think he was capable of that kind of cruelty. But that didn't change the fact that Shana was the girl he loved and admired. In some way that made him implicitly guilty by association.

"I dumped Shana on the spot—in front of everybody," Max announced. "I had been planning to break up with her anyway . . . just not in front of a roomful of people."

Huh. That I hadn't expected.

Max was quiet for a moment. "Jane, you asked me to metamorphose you into the kind of girl a guy like me would go for, but that girl was there all along. *I'm* the one who needed to change, to become the kind of guy that a girl like *you* would go for."

"I . . . I . . ." No words would come. Was he really saying these things, or was I having one of my usual fantasies?

He smiled. "I guess we've both learned a lesson through all of this, huh? I'm in love with you, Jane," Max said simply, taking a couple of steps toward me. "And there's a tiny little part of me that's still holding out a flicker of hope that maybe, just maybe, you're in love with me too."

I felt a hot tear slide down my cheek. But for the first time I understood what people meant when they said they had cried tears of joy. I had never been so incredibly happy in my life.

And this wasn't a joke. And it wasn't part of our

deal, or our bargain, or whatever Max and I had called our strange relationship. This was *us,* two people who understood each other better than anyone else in the world. I knew that with every iota of my being.

"I love you too, Max," I whispered.

The next second he was pulling me into his arms. I smelled the rugged scent of his soap, felt the soft cotton of his shirt against my cheek. This was the best moment of my life. But I was so shocked that all I could do was hold Max tight.

He pulled away, placing his hands on either side of my face. "Jane Smith, will you make me the happiest guy in the world by agreeing to go to the prom with me?"

I couldn't speak. I just nodded, gazing into those hazel eyes. I knew I was grinning like a lunatic, but I didn't care. I knew Max understood. Just like he understood everything else about me.

"I'll take that as a yes," Max murmured. And then he slid his arms to my waist and pulled me against him.

Max's lips captured mine, and it was as if my dream had literally come true. His kiss was warm, and then hot, and then it melted my very bones. We kissed on and on, unable to get enough of each other. I felt his touch to my toes, and I never wanted to let go.

The worst night of my life had just turned into the best night of my life. And all of it had happened while I was *me.* The same plain old Jane Smith—in the same jeans and T-shirt and ponytail—I had been forever. Best of all, I was the girl I *wanted* to be, and I was in love with a guy who wanted that girl too!

"This is what it's all about," Max whispered into my ear when we finally broke apart. "*You're* what it's all about."

"Thank you, Max," I whispered back. "Thank you for helping me realize that I never needed to change at all."

Then his lips found mine again. And we didn't say anything else for a long, long time. . . .

*Do you ever wonder about falling in love? About members of the opposite sex? Do you need a little friendly advice but have no one to turn to? Well, that's where we come in . . . Jenny and Jake. Send us those questions you're dying to ask, and we'll give you the straight scoop on life and love.*

## DEAR JAKE

**Q:** *Help! I'm so confused. I can't tell if the guy I like (Anthony) is a jerk or not! One minute he's sweet to me, and the next minute he's totally harsh and making fun of me to the point of bringing me to tears. There never seems to be a reason for his sudden change of attitude. Why does he turn so hot and cold? Should I just stay away from him?*

**MS, Rapid City, SD**

**A:** Trying to figure out Mr. Mixed Messages will drive you crazy. Your best bet is to tell your crush how you feel about his behavior—and see how he reacts and responds. If he's willing to talk about why he's nice to you during lunch period but a jerk after English class (coughing up an apology and an explanation too), that's a good sign. If he pretends not to know what you're talking about, then perhaps he's not so crush-worthy, after all.

**Q:** *How can I get an older guy to notice me? I've had a major crush on Brett forever, but he's three years older than I am, and he treats me as though I were his little sister! He even ruffled my hair last week as he passed me on the street. I'm thirteen, so it's not like I'm a kid anymore. Should I try to dress sexier for him? Talk to him about more sophisticated stuff? There have to be some surefire things I can do to get him to fall for me.*

**PS, Porter, ME**

**A:** There's really only one surefire thing you can do: Be yourself. I know, I know: That's not what you wanted to hear. But it's the best advice I can give you on how to attract the guy you like. Besides, trying to look or act "older" is very hard work and no fun at all; after all, you're pretending to be someone you're not. So if a guy likes you based on that, he's not really getting to know the real you. If it's any help, it sounds as though Brett likes you just fine. So just keep being yourself!

# DEAR JENNY

**Q:** *I've got a huge problem. I've been dating Scott for a few months and we like each other a lot. But, I'm starting to like a friend of his (Garrett). I find myself daydreaming about Garrett in class, during dinner, even while I'm brushing my teeth! I really* *like my boyfriend, so should I try to forget my feelings for Garrett? My friend told me the only way to get Garrett out of my system is to hook up with him. But I'm not sure about kissing another guy when I have a boyfriend. What should I do?*

*MC, Athens, GA*

**A:** Before you do anything, spend some time sorting through your feelings. Ask yourself a bunch of questions, and you might be surprised to learn that you have all the answers you need. For instance, do you really like Garrett, or is it just an innocent crush? Do you want to get to know him—or do you just like checking him out? Are you happy with your boyfriend? Is there a problem in your relationship with Scott that could use talking over? Once you've really thought things through, you'll have a clearer idea of how you really feel. And, if you still aren't sure, remember this: You can always get to know Garrett as a friend and then make your decision.

**Q:** *I don't want to sound like a snob, but I'm really popular and practically lead the in-crowd. My problem is that I like a boy who's not popular at all. He doesn't fit into any of the usual clique categories. He's not a brain or a nerd or a stoner or a jock, etc. He's got a great sense of humor, and I think he's really nice and cute. Because I like him so much, I've stopped caring that he's not part of my crowd. But if my friends knew I liked him, they'd make fun of me. Please don't tell me that means they're not really my* *friends. Being popular is important to me, but so is this boy. Help!*

**GU, West Jordan, UT**

**A:** Okay, okay, I won't lecture you on the meaning of friendship. But I will suggest that perhaps you're not giving yourself—or your friends—enough credit. What makes you so sure they'll laugh at you for liking a boy who isn't part of your crowd? Give your buds a chance, and give yourself a chance to follow your heart.

*Do you have any questions about love?*
*Although we can't respond individually to your letters,*
*you just might find your questions answered in our column.*
*Write to:*
Jenny Burgess or Jake Korman
c/o 17th Street Productions, Inc.
33 West 17th Street
New York, NY 10011

# Don't miss any of the books in *Love Stories*
## —the romantic series from Bantam Books!